MW01068662

THE DESPERADO DAYS

X.C. ATKINS

THE DES...

DAYS

THE DESPERADO DAYS

TRNSFR BOOKS, *Grand Rapids*

PUBLISHED BY TRNSFR BOOKS

TRNSFRBOOKS.COM

LIBRARY OF CONGRESS CONTROL NUMBER: 2022936133

ISBN 978-1-7355727-4-1 (PAPERBACK)

ISBN 978-1-7355727-5-8 (E-BOOK)

BOOK DESIGN BY ALBAN FISCHER

PRINTED IN THE UNITED STATES OF AMERICA

DISTRIBUTED BY SMALL PRESS DISTRIBUTION: SPDBOOKS.ORG

FIRST EDITION

CONTENTS

THE DESPERADO DAYS

THE WORLD

I shoved the door open, hard. It smacked violently against the wall, but at that moment, it might as well have made no sound. The music inside blared unbelievably loud. It always seems like more can go wrong when there's loud music.

"Where the fuck is he," I said.

Gigi was sitting on a stool holding a rag up to her face. The rag was bloody. Maria stood next to her.

"He went out the back," she said.

"I didn't ask you to come here," Gigi said.

"No, you didn't. Maria did. You got your head too far up your ass to know what's good for you."

I was about to pass the kitchen on my way to the back, but an idea jumped in my head. I went into the kitchen and grabbed a roller I saw on the counter, then continued on out the back. The screen door still hung open. The patio light buzzed, bugs crackling against it like tiny bolts of lightning. Jimmy stood in the yard, smoking a cigarette. When he saw me, he flicked the cigarette away.

"Listen, asshole, she had it coming."

"So do you," I said.

I cracked him good on the top of the head with the roller and he said ow and he punched me straight in the gut. My wind came out and I took a knee, but I knew better, so I punched him in the ball sack. He took a seat against the fence behind him. I started looking for the roller. I'd lost it. I didn't remember losing it but I wasn't holding it anymore.

"You think you're some kind of superhero, huh?"

We started rolling around in the dirt. I was punching his ribs like I was trying to punch a hole in the sky. He bit my ear and pulled up and a piece of my ear went with him. I could feel all the blood going down my neck. A fist went right in between my eyes and I went blind. More fists rained down, but I couldn't move my arms anymore to do anything about it. Finally, it stopped and so did time. It was just me and the ground and the air bulging in my belly like a jellyfish.

Small hands picked me up.

"Jesus. We gotta take him to the hospital."

I hated the hospital, but I still couldn't see, so I let those hands hold me up.

"Nobody asked you to go after him like that," I heard Gigi say.

"Nah," I said through my split lips. "You don't ever ask for shit. You just sit around complaining all the time how the world does you wrong."

IDOLS PART FOUR

I was at work, leaning on a counter in the server station, eating some bread and butter. I was so poor those days I had to schedule when I ate around when I went to work. You see, instead of spending my meager tips and non-existent wage on proper groceries, I spent it all on booze, gas, and late nights at Aladdin's, the local pizza joint owned by a family of Middle Easterners. We never asked them where exactly.

I either went with two slices of pepperoni or the calzone. Calzone if I was thinking ahead. Waking up to a leftover calzone the next day could be a nice little treat. On rare nights, I'd even splurge and get some garlic knots and marinara. I was still young; the carbs weren't hitting yet.

But I was at work, and standing beside me was Pip, and he was slurping down a Mountain Dew from a kiddie cup. He was a lot taller than me but also a lot younger, even though I was pretty young too. Years feel different in your twenties. They still seem to spread in a way that a year or two can mean a lot.

Anyway, he was one of those young kids that moves up fast. Maybe because he just laughed at everything and wasn't a complete dipshit when it came to common motor skills. He didn't screw up often and he showed up, which at the end of the day was all the bosses really wanted. He was just one of those humans tailor-made to be the manager of something. A shoe store or an office or a bank. Guys like him got their pictures put in a frame and hung on a wall and always came from good-hearted families and always got way too trashed at work parties but not in a way that might ruin their marriage. Not usually. Regardless, none of us were that far along anyway.

I did like Pip even though I picked on him often. I think he kind of looked up to me. That was a new thing for me at the time. But I was getting used to it quick. I'd just use my older brother's lines and watch them work like a charm. If you could see me now, old boy.

Sophie walked in to join us, and she put her tray on the counter dramatically and sighed loudly, not saying anything but clearly in that way I'd learned a woman wants you to ask what's wrong.

I still liked Sophie so I bit. Otherwise, I'd just have walked out the room and minded my business.

"What now?" I asked.

"This girl is back in the restaurant and she was just here yesterday and she was an absolute terror but then on top of all that she didn't tip and now she just got sat in my section again today," she ranted.

"What table?"

"Twenty-seven."

Pip and I went to the edge of the server station and stuck our heads out to take a look. Just a normal looking girl. I mean, she was black, but I'd already debunked that theory many times for my white colleagues. For any black customer they got shit from, I could show them a white soccer mom, an Asian college kid, an Indian husband and father of four, a set of teenagers. Everyone had the potential to be shit. But so did everyone have the potential for you to turn them and make them a mark. For you to bend them by the wiles of your charisma. I had confidence in this by then. It was the game. And we all played the game, whether we liked it or not. We all played the game, or we got played by the game.

I turned to Sophie. "I'll take the table."

"What?" she said in disbelief.

"I'll take the table. Watch this. I'm gonna give her the best damn service she ever got in her life. And if she stiffs me too, she'll know like hell about it."

Pip cheered me on. I grabbed Sophie's tray and whirled out onto the floor, chest puffed, apron immaculate, stubble on my chin right at the length I'd deemed ruggedly handsome. I came up to the girl's table. She was with a friend. I greeted them warmly, keeping strong eye contact, and they put on big smiles. In my mind, I was already telling myself: piece of cake.

Don't get me wrong, I wasn't thinking I was going to make millions off this young lady. I was looking for the basic tip. I was just looking to not get stiffed. Bare minimum. I just wanted to prove a point. And the time came for the check to be put down and she smiled again, and I was brimming with certainty in my talents.

From the sides of my eyes, I watched her put money in the checkbook and I went to pick it up and said brightly, "I'll be right back with the change."

I left and returned, and this time, Pip, Sophie and I all watched her, very covert style, take all the bills and all the change from the checkbook and dump it into her purse. She left nothing. We waited a few more moments, just in case she were to add something after all. She did not.

"She's doing it. See? She's doing it," Sophie said.

"She's doing it, Levy," Pip repeated. "What are you gonna do?"

I clenched my teeth. I didn't look at either of them. I kept my sight on the young lady. Then I beelined it straight to her.

It was busy that lunch. Every table around her was occupied. I didn't give a damn. I picked up the checkbook right in front of her and I opened it and held it open, to emphasize the imminent point, to really make this climatic.

"Really? You're gonna do this two days in a row? You're gonna come into the restaurant and stiff us two days in a row? Wow. Wow. Unreal. Unbelievable."

I snapped the checkbook shut with a sound that resembled me just as well slapping her in the face. Bap! The look on her face! Now that was priceless. She and her friend both stared at me, mouths agape, mortified. The people at the tables around us snapped their necks, looking at me, then the girls, shocked, bystanders to the humiliating scene. A knowing and judgmental disgust began to well on their faces. Non-tippers, their faces said. Shame. Shame!

The desired effect achieved, I swung around, and walked back into the safety of the server station where their eyes could not follow.

"Levy! I can't believe you did that!" Sophie just about screamed. She hugged me ferociously. Pip held up his hand for a fiver and I slapped the hell out of it. He waved it off painfully but still grinned ear to ear. Then we crept back to the edge of the station to look and see what would happen next.

The young lady had left the restaurant, but we could see her standing just outside, gesturing wildly to her friend who was talking back just as animatedly. They did that for a while. Then she started to head back to the restaurant.

"Oh fuck," I said.

Of all the possible futures my actions may have produced, I hadn't considered this one.

I walked real fast into the back of the restaurant, the dry storage. I was visualizing my impending future more accurately now.

She was going to ask for the manager.

Dominick was the manager today.

I was gonna get fucking fired.

Now, it wasn't that Dominick hated me. Dominick had hired

me. Dominick was slicker than eel shit, and it wasn't just the stuff he put in his hair. He was savvy. He was older. He just knew things we didn't. Dominick had already been a hot shot. And now he was assistant general manager. He had a family and a wife and he didn't stand for any disrespect from his young and reckless employees. He was ruthless but could simultaneously sit right amongst us and joke around and the jokes wouldn't be corny. They'd actually be pretty funny. Which made us all even more uneasy. Because we didn't know whether to love him dearly or fear him out right. The reality was, he wanted both of those things. And that made him very dangerous.

I stood in the dry storage and awaited my fate. And fate is never late. He stepped in that room with me, and even though he was a good couple inches shorter than me, he might as well have been touching the ceiling with his masterfully gelled, shoulder length hair.

"Levy," he said through gritted teeth. "What … did you … do?"

"Listen, Dom …"

"NO. YOU LISTEN. BOY. Let me tell you something. For starters, people don't like you, Levy. Do you know that? And I'm really beginning to understand why. Do you know I have to fight to keep you on the schedule? You work hard, Levy. I know that. But your coworkers all think you're a mean little shit, and that you think you're better than everyone else. So I'm going to tell you something. You're not better than anyone. You've been hanging on a thread this whole damn time. And I got a pair of scissors for your ass."

He stepped closer to me. I took a step back.

"Let me tell you what you did today. You fucked us. You fucked all of us." He waved a finger around in a circle when he said that. "You think of yourself as some type of hero? Pulling a stunt like that? But you know what you really did? You just made sure that . . ." here he swallowed thickly and cleared his throat, pointing back out the room, "that young lady is going to come back and make the next person suffer. And maybe another one after that. Because she came back in here and demanded I fire your ass. And maybe I should. But what I did right at that moment was I promised her a bunch of free shit. Because that's what we do here. We use free shit like a Band-Aid. And now she's gonna come back here with that free shit and use it, and make the next person suffer. And the next person suffer. Just because you thought you could humiliate this person. And for what? For five fucking dollars? You so hard up that you gotta get yourself fired for five dollars? Do you want to be fired, is that it?"

"No, Dom. I don't. I really don't," I said, unable to lift my eyes off the ground and untuck my tail from my crotch.

That's when I felt his hand on my shoulder. I looked up. His face wasn't red anymore. "I know you thought you were proving some kind of point or sticking up for your coworkers, or whatever bullshit noble thing you thought you were doing. But sometimes, you have to be wise and understand when to pick your battles. Sometimes you need to understand what's worth it and what's not. I do think you're a good worker, Levy. But shit like this will come back to bite you on your ass more often than not. There's a time to stand up for your dignity and there's a time to swallow your pride and get on to the next one. That five dollars you didn't get from her is five dollars you'd make up with the next table. I see you out there. Your coworkers might not all like you but the guests do. And I think you know that. You always make high sales and you know the menu. You're fast and you're not sloppy. You could do well in this business. But you gotta be smart. So try to think a couple of steps ahead, or else you'll always be putting yourself behind. You hear me?"

I could have cried. My face was breaking up and my shoulders were shaking. I felt like I was turning twelve years old. I just nodded my head, trembling, and said, "Yeah, Dom. Yeah. Thank you."

"Now clock out and go home."

"I'm fired?"

"No. I just don't want to look at your face the rest of today. And when you come back in here tomorrow, boy, you better have shaved."

JUKEBOX MAGIC

I'd finally gotten this girl at work to come out and get a drink with me. I'd been working on her forever. She was super pretty and if she wore heels she'd probably be a lot taller than me. Thankfully that night she was wearing boots. It was winter in Philadelphia.

I didn't really have any business hanging out with girls that looked this nice but then again, I never thought things like that ever applied to me. That shit's just a state of mind. It was only ever really about how you walked anyway right? I went for it and if it didn't work out, whatever. Otherwise, I went for it. Just for the hell of it. I had time.

She had long straight auburn hair and she was from California. I'd been to San Diego once. Slept on a floor with three other dudes, getting drunk for a week. That was a long time ago. Now I was living in Philly doing things in my dad's hometown I'd never tell him about. I really wasn't talking to too many people in the first place. A lot of times, I felt like I was hiding. There were a lot of places to do that in Philadelphia. I was hiding and trying to figure out who I was. What I was becoming. Somehow figuring all that out involved spending a lot of time with the ladies. Or no one at all.

There was a bar not far from work that had a pool table and no windows. I was really getting into the Philly dive bar scene at the time but hadn't figured out there were some girls you could take to these sort of places and some girls you ought not to.

We got some looks but mostly the coast was clear.

The bartender asked for her ID. He didn't bother with me. I'd been in there enough and was one of the few patrons generous enough to put money in the juke, otherwise everyone would just stew miserably in silence, listening to the shot glasses kiss the wood grain.

I ordered a Special. You lived in Philly, you knew that meant a beer and a shot. What beer and a shot it was changed for each bar, but I was always the same animal. The bartender looked at the girl. She was looking around for something and wasn't finding it.

"Um," she said.

The bartender knocked his knuckle on the counter and walked away.

"Sorry," she said to me, grinning, but not really in a way I found cute. I'd been judgmental from a young age.

"Take your time," I said, looking for a window to look out of, and not finding one.

She finally ordered an IPA. I paid the man and we took a seat on some stools with a table between us along the wall. I walked over with my beer and shot of whiskey and before I sat down, I took down the shot. Very casually. She kind of looked a little horrified when I did. Like how someone looks when you take a bite out of your dinner without saying grace. Except I wasn't raised with religion. I could understand walking into someone's home and taking my shoes off but, yeah, I guess you could say I had no reserve in the indulging department of life. Not in a place like this. I was here to play the part.

"So you're in school?" I asked politely.

"Yeah," she said.

The conversation went like that. Dumb and lifeless. She started getting on her phone a lot. When she did, I'd looked around, still trying to find a window, even though the bar having no windows or televisions was what I liked about it. Eventually, my eyeballs would land back on her. She was very pretty to look at but we both kept looking around hoping someone would save us. And in a way, that's sort of what happened.

"You mind if my girlfriend joins us?"

At first, that irritated me, because who wanted to be a third wheel, which I knew had become my sudden destiny, but I said, "Yeah, sure. More the merrier."

I went up and got myself another round. She wasn't even halfway done with her drink yet.

It didn't take long for her friend to arrive. It was hard to look good next to my coworker, which was why she was the first thing you saw when you walked into the restaurant. But her friend was cute. She was all right. She shook my hand on the intro, sizing me up respectfully. Then she ordered a drink, tipped, and joined us at the table. I brought along a stool for her and she thanked me without any fuss.

"I like this place," she said.

"Wow, you've been here before?" my coworker asked, surprised.

"Yeah. Decent pool table. Good jukebox. Speaking of, any of our party holding cash? I suddenly feel like it's our responsibility to put some life into this place," she said, standing up.

I looked at her in awe, my mouth a little open and my eyebrows raised. Then I reached into my pocket and pulled out a fiver. I handed it to her. She grinned, taking it and heading to the juke. I watched her. Then I looked at my coworker. She was staring at me. I closed my mouth and nodded with the utmost grace.

The first song was "Brass in Pocket." A safe choice and always a winner. She started swaying, glowing in the light of the juke. She finished her picks and rejoined us. She seemed satisfied with her selection. I was looking forward to listening to them. The girls started talking about some mutual friends. I leaned back against the wall, feeling good that I was hanging out with two pretty girls.

By the time my coworker had finished her first beer, her friend and I were ready to do another as well. Her friend was ordering whiskey and ginger ales. The music seemed to lighten up the bartender. He even told us a joke.

"What do you call cheese that isn't yours? Nacho cheese."

I slapped the bar, laughing. We went back over to our little table.

"I still got some tracks available on the juke," the friend said to me. "Why don't you go pick some?"

"What if I pick songs you already picked?"

"Then we'll know we both got good taste."

Fucking A, I thought. I went over to the jukebox. I tried to pick some deep cuts. Some tracks off the beaten path, but would still be winners. When I turned to rejoin the girls, they were standing up and dancing together, giggling. Some of the old men at the bar were taking looks over their shoulders. Hell yeah, I thought.

I took my seat against the wall and watched them happily. My coworker motioned me to join them, so I did. The three of us danced. We were having fun. The music sounded better that night than it ever had in that place.

My coworker had to go to the bathroom. She skipped to the back of the bar, appearing more like a little girl, just inside a woman's body. Her beautiful dusky hair bounced with her, in and out of the light. Her friend and I kept dancing, her face down so that her hair covered her eyes, a single hand in the air. The next song came on. It was a slower one, a good one. It was a song where I'd put my hands on my partner's hips and she'd put her arms around my shoulders. I thought her friend would sit down for this one, or just do something else. But she stepped forward, and without thinking about it, I did what I felt I should do in that sort of situation. We started dancing silently. I mean, we didn't say anything. But it felt like everything was very very loud. In the best way. The absolute best way. A little way into the song, she laid her head on my chest. I totally forgot where we were, where we came from. I was all ready to sail into the cosmos.

The song wasn't even over, and someone slapped the shit out of the back of my head. It was loud, and it stung me back into reality. I reared around ready to breathe fire. But it was just my coworker. She had a surprised look on her face, like she didn't believe it either, but her face was also red. I could see she was mad. But she'd still surprised herself. Me and her friend too. Her friend just kind of stood there like, "Shit." My coworker beelined it to the door.

I looked at her friend. We were both stunned. Speechless. Finally, she sighed, grabbed both her and my coworker's jacket, and started walking out too. Then, just at the end of the bar, she said something to the bartender. He handed her a pen. She wrote something down on a napkin and folded it in half. She turned around, held it up to me, laid it on the bar, and left.

I walked up to where she'd set it on the bar. An old geezer was reaching for it. I slapped his wrist and he retracted his withered claw. I picked up the napkin and unfolded it. Her number. The name "Simone" written on top.

NO RADIO

On the weekdays, Elmer Vasquez always woke up before the rest of his family, whether he had work or not. He went to the bathroom, washed his face and his teeth, regarded his ever-receding hair line, then went into the kitchen and made himself a bowl of cereal. It was winter, there was hardly ever any light, and it seemed like everywhere he stepped in the house the floor would creak. It was an old house in a part of Newport News, Virginia, that the TV told him was just getting worse and worse.

It was usually between 6 and 6:30 a.m. that he got the call on whether he'd be needed for work or not. He'd sit there at the table next to the phone, waiting, and picked it up as soon as it rang. That way his wife and daughter weren't bothered. If he was called in, he rarely worked in town. Work usually took him a couple hours out. Sometimes farther.

Elmer worked for a guy named Buster, and Buster had a company that worked for cheap and did anything from extermination to carpentry to welding. Elmer knew how to do all these things and if he didn't know, he'd learn it by the end of the day and usually the people were none the wiser. The clientele were almost always rich and white and couldn't give two fucks.

He was finishing his bowl of Captain Crunch when the phone rang.

"Hello?"

"Morning, Elmer."

"Morning, Buster."

"Gonna need you to go out to Williamsburg today. Lady says she's got termites. You know the routine. Then when you're done, drive down to Phoebus so you can install some windows to a house. He's already got the windows. If you need to get anything extra, hit the Lowe's and we'll tack it on to his bill. I'll text you the addresses."

"OK, Buster."

The job paid but it didn't pay anything crazy. Enough to keep the house, have a decent car and a truck, cable TV, keep his family fed. His wife and daughter.

Life hadn't been a hell of a lot easier before the kid, who was a year and a half now, but somehow he felt as if it had been. His wife, Esperanza, stayed at home. She took care of the kid and cooked for them and kept the house up. He looked around the place and shook his head. Yeah, real nice and tidy, my ass. He still had to mow the lawn, but at least this time of year the mosquitoes quit.

He had a shed in the yard big enough to have a couple fellas over for ping-pong. That night his buddy Tony came over with a friend he could barely just remember from high school. His name was Levy and he was visiting from out of town.

Levy hadn't changed much since high school. It'd been about eight years. His jeans were too tight. He seemed full of remarkable energy.

Eight years. Elmer looked down at his belly. In high school, he'd had a full head of hair. Sharp shape-ups. Expensive sneakers. He played basketball almost every day and dated lots of girls.

He didn't hate his life. He just didn't see a whole lot of upside in it for him. He loved his wife, but she'd put on a lot of weight and wasn't doing anything to get rid of it. They both probably bored each other to death. If they ever fought, and that was very rare these days, it was usually just a whole lot of her going on and him staring at a wall, usually in the end consenting to whatever her grief was. He loved his daughter, but many times he was too tired to play with her. When she got upset, it scared him and he'd quickly hand her over to her mother. It was a stage of her life, he would admit to himself only, that he was hoping she would grow out of quickly.

In the shed, they didn't talk very much at all at first, playing their matches seriously, drinking to keep warm. The shed was as cold as if they were standing in the yard. But soon the beer started to work. Levy started talking to Tony about an idea he had for the both of them to go to the Keys. Elmer was sitting on a bar stool, watching them play.

"Couple of months from now, you know, right before spring hits, and it's still pretty cool up here, it'd be the perfect time to go down," Levy said. "Good night life, plenty of bars, music just pouring out of the bars, women wiggling around. Holy moly."

"Sounds fun," Tony agreed.

Levy played too aggressively. His slams often completely missed the table. He was only still in the game because Tony would get too comfortable. Elmer and Tony played a lot of ping-pong together. It was usually pretty even.

"Plus, I've always wanted to go see Hemingway's house."

"The writer?" Elmer asked.

"That's right. It's kind of a tourist attraction and it's supposed to be filled with cats, which I'm not very excited about, but it's something I have to see. Just sort of to say I did."

Game point, advantage Tony. Levy served. The volley lasted just long enough to make it a little exciting, but finally Tony just slipped it over the net and Levy couldn't catch it in time. Levy was loud but Elmer didn't mind because there usually wasn't a whole lot of noise around here. It was a nice change for once.

Tony handed Elmer the paddle.

"Y'all two play. I'm tired of beating the both of you," Tony said.

"You've only beat me once tonight, homie. Barely." He took the paddle and walked over to his side of the table.

"Ping it?" he asked Levy.

"Sure."

They both drank deeply from their cans, emptied them, and began the next round.

"So what," Elmer asked, "y'all would just go down there and party?"

"There's other things to do," Levy said. "We could fish, I bet. You fish, Elmer?"

"I love to fish."

"You do any fishing around here?"

"Not as much as I'd like. When I ain't working, I'm so damn tired, I just want to sit on the couch and watch TV all day."

"That's not good for you," Levy said. "You oughta get out on the bay, find a river, get you a boat."

"Get a boat?" Elmer said, smacking the ball so that it went completely left of the table, hitting the ground next to Tony's feet.

"Yeah, why not? Just a little one. Save up for it. People act like they don't know how to save anymore. Buy one for cheap. Shit, I bet you could fix it up right here in this shed. You got the room."

"He's right, man," Tony said, tossing him the ball. "Put a little money aside, do something with that money besides buying DVDs and video games. Wouldn't take very long. You know you could fix one up. I'd even help you out."

Elmer knew Tony would help out too. Tony was in a similar line of business with the carpentry and handyman type deal. Elmer thought about it a while. Suddenly, he could see the boat propped up in here. See himself sanding it, painting it, naming it after his dog that just died. His dog's name was Chip. He'd been hit by a car.

"Game point. Your serve," Levy said, tapping the ball across the table to him.

It was twenty to eleven. Elmer had been playing terribly. He served. Levy hit it back to him to the opposite corner of the table. Elmer jumped to that side and sent it back. Levy then hit it back to the other side, skimming the edge. Elmer didn't get there in time.

"That's game. And that was a beating too," Tony said. "You must be losing your touch, Elmer."

"Maybe he just needs to drink more," Levy said, "Get back on, Tone."

∎

Elmer had a number of jobs he did where he was paid under the table. He figured if he gave all his paychecks to his wife, for every third job he did under the table, he'd put the money aside to start saving up for the boat. He would save up for one, buy it for cheap, and fix it right up in the shed. He started picking up every job he could. He was away from the house more, but he didn't mind that.

He couldn't imagine Esperanza getting upset with him for wanting to get a boat, and didn't feel it necessary to tell her right away what he was doing. He knew he'd never be able to do something like leave town with a buddy and party like old times. That was definitely something Esperanza would flip out over, and the energy he'd expend even trying to argue his case would already make it not worth it. Besides, he'd genuinely feel bad for leaving her that way. His wife never left the house without him or their daughter unless it was to the grocery store or to buy clothes. She didn't have any friends and her family had moved a few years after high school.

She knew he liked to fish, and this would keep him relatively close to home. Just this little boat to go out on the bay with on Sunday mornings. She'd let him do that. He hadn't been motivated to do something since before they had their daughter, and that was more a motivation bred out of necessity.

Thinking all day about it, Elmer came home and found his wife in the living room standing over their daughter, who was sitting on the floor playing with a doll. He came up behind her and wrapped his arms around her and kissed her behind the ear.

She turned around quickly and gave him a look as if he had terrible news. But when she saw his face her expression half faded away and all she said was, "What are you doing?"

"Nothing, baby." His hands fell to his side. "What are we having for dinner?"

■

Months went by. He was watching the money set aside grow in his savings account. He started buying magazines, taking home newspapers, researching boats, looking for deals. He played more energetically with his daughter Isis, and realized that when she laughed, she reminded him of himself.

The only thing that didn't add up was that Esperanza seemed different. She talked less when he came home from work and when they did have a conversation it was always about something he needed to do around the house or to ask questions about his day that seemed to him as though she were suspicious of something he was doing.

Finally, he decided to tell her.

"I'm going to buy a boat."

"You're going to buy a boat? What do you mean you're buying a boat?"

"I'm gonna buy one!" he laughed.

"How the hell you gonna do that? With what money?"

"I've been saving money," he told her.

"Saving what money?!"

"I've been putting aside money. Nothing that would take away from anything. Just a little bit, here and there. It isn't hurting us. Besides, what the hell does it matter what I do with my money? It's my money. I earn it. Don't I put food on the table?"

"How do you think we can afford a boat?" she asked him.

"It's my money! Aren't the bills getting paid? Don't we have food to eat?"

"We can do something else with the money. We could go on a vacation or something. What the hell do we need with a boat?"

Elmer could feel himself getting ready to boil over. She knew he had a bad temper. It rarely came out anymore but their fights used to be terrible and he hated himself afterwards, but not enough to stop himself if she took him to the point. Isis was in the other room watching TV, so he held himself back. He wanted to really give it to her.

"You listen to me," he said in a monotone voice. "This is my goddamn money. I wake up every morning and I work my ass off for this money and it's all for you and Isis. What the hell do I have? When was the last time I went out with some of my friends for a good time?"

"With who? Tony? What the hell are you going to do with him? He's still living at his mother's house!"

"Yeah, and I'm jealous of him! Cause he doesn't have to worry about coming home to this shit every day! He isn't miserable every day of his damn life! I'm sick of this! I'm getting a fucking boat and if you don't like it you can get the hell out!"

Isis started crying from the other room. They'd been yelling loudly by that point. He left both of them in the house, slamming the door after him. He got into his truck and called Tony. Tony told him he was just getting out of the shower. He was about to go to dinner with a girl, Tony said. Elmer said OK and told him to have fun. He turned the car on anyway and drove to the next city, parking in a lot that looked down to the James River. There he fell asleep.

When he woke up, it was the hour before he normally received the call from Buster to let him know if he had any work. But he wasn't at home.

He rushed to get back. He kept looking in his rearview, expecting a cop to find him speeding. But he got home without any trouble. He was passing the bathroom on the way to the kitchen and saw Esperanza sitting on the floor next to the toilet. He stopped and looked down at her, stepping closer.

"Hey . . . what's the matter with you?" he asked.

"Nothing," she said.

"Are you sick?"

"I'll be fine," she said.

He was concerned for her but he was still irritated from last night. He stood there a moment, looking at her.

"Did Buster call?"

"I don't know. Maybe."

"Jesus," Elmer said, and walked away to the kitchen.

■

He didn't say anything to Esperanza outside a few words for a couple of weeks after that, and the conversation was always about Isis or bills. She barely spoke to him either. They avoided eye contact, and when it happened accidentally, like bumping into each other in the hall, the encounter almost felt painful. But he wouldn't change his mind. He wouldn't apologize. That's the last thing I'll do, he told himself.

He continued his search for the perfect cheap boat. He really wanted to spend time working on it, but he didn't want it to be complete crap either. He began to use the computer he'd bought for his wife. He never used the thing, still typed with his index fingers, it took forever to get to the right websites, but he didn't get frustrated. This was something new, and he welcomed it. A whole world was opening up to him.

His wife would pass silently behind him at times while he was on the computer. He'd hardly notice her unless she was making prolonged noise. Then he would turn around and snarl, "Could you quiet down? Between you and Isis I can't get any goddamn peace in this house!"

It was really the only time he was negative anymore. It almost felt like his wife had just become some type of roommate and they kept different schedules and when they occupied the same room it was awkward and someone had to leave after a while. His money continued to accumulate and inside himself he could feel the excitement building, it was all he ever thought about, all he talked about when Tony came over to play ping-pong in the shed.

One of those nights Elmer came to bed late after spending time with Tony. He felt just fine from the beer. Esperanza was already in bed. The room was dark. He sat on his side of the bed. The mattress sagged down. He took off his shoes, tossed them towards the closet. They made thud sounds, unmistakable. He took off his shirt and pants and threw them too. He burped and got into bed.

Pulling on some of the blankets, he began to hear Esperanza crying. She was crying very, very quietly, but he could feel her little shakes in bed, hear her breathing that way. He listened to her for a while.

A few minutes passed by and Elmer asked her, "What's wrong?" She didn't answer.

"Hey," he turned around in the bed, to face her in the dark. "Baby, what's wrong?"

She didn't say anything.

"Well, if you can't say anything and you want to cry, can you do that in the other room? I gotta go to sleep. You know I gotta wake up early."

He waited for a moment. Then she got up from the bed and walked out of the bedroom, leaving the door open after her. The sound of her walking on the creaking floor became faint as she disappeared in the dark. He fell asleep quickly.

■

Less than a month to go is what he figured. He had a small pile of boating magazines in the shed. He knew he'd go for a skiff of some sort. Flat bottom. Fiberglass, because the wood would rot quicker. Elmer thought about the money he had in his savings account. It'd felt good to see the money grow. The only thing that would feel better was spending it.

He was driving home from Norfolk on 64 and the roads were backed up as usual. Traffic was almost always terrible around here, which was a wonder, because really there was nowhere to go. Nowhere except work and home. It's all anyone ever went. Maybe a Red Lobster here, a movie there. Take the kids to Chuck E. Cheese. Isis was just coming to that age, and soon he'd be one of those haggard jackasses hunched down in there eating pizza and hitting plastic pop-ups with foam hammers, spending tokens on arcade games that weren't nearly as fun as the ones he'd grown up playing.

He didn't listen to the radio when he drove. Not that he never listened to music ever, but when he was just on the road, going or coming back from work, he didn't bother. No radio helped him to think more. The silence occupied his transit more peacefully versus constantly shifting through stations, trying to find a song that didn't make him want to ram the car next to him. And he thought about all kinds of things. His life, his wife, his daughter, Tony, high school, the shape of the house, the yard, his older brother that lived in Maryland, other women, whether or not he should get more job security and go work for the shipyard. Funny thing was, as soon as he stepped out of the truck, all those thoughts vanished right into thin air, as if he hadn't been driving for however long, thinking about it all.

He got home and walked into the house and Esperanza was in the kitchen and it smelled good in there. Isis was in the living room playing with a stuffed walrus. He set his bag down and took off his jacket and placed it on the hook next to the door and took off his boots and walked into the kitchen. He opened the fridge, then stopped himself and went over to the sink to wash his hands. After he finished toweling them dry, he returned to the fridge and got out a beer and plopped himself down on a chair in the kitchen. He watched Esperanza work. This was a peaceful thing for him too. She had a Coca-Cola in one hand and a spatula in the other. They didn't say a word.

She was putting the finishing touches on the meal. Chicken, green beans, rice. Simple. Esperanza put Isis in the highchair and

Elmer gave a blessing and they started in. Isis made cheerful sounds. Esperanza was a good mother, Elmer thought. I gotta give her that. Maybe I should tell her some time, he realized. He went on eating.

They finished dinner and Esperanza collected the dishes and put them in the sink and started washing them. Isis went back into the living room with her toys, television playing. He grabbed another beer, his third, and before walking out of the kitchen he said, "Good chicken tonight."

He went into the living room and laid out on the couch. Isis was watching cartoons. He didn't understand any of the cartoons of her day. They were nothing like the cartoons he grew up with. There was no violence or futuristic robots or dinosaurs or swords. Just a bunch of weird graphics bouncing around. What kind of kids were his daughter's generation going to grow up to be? He fell asleep on the couch without coming up with an answer.

■

He woke himself up to find he was still on the couch. The TV was off and he was alone. He got up, very slowly, aching, and knocked over the beer he'd set on the floor. It was only a little left that spilled out. He picked up the can and stepped into the kitchen and tossed it into the trashcan.

Sluggishly, he brought himself upstairs to the bedroom. He undressed and sat on his side of the bed. Esperanza moaned.

"Go back to sleep, baby. I fell asleep on the couch," he said.

"I'm not feeling good," she said.

"What is it now?"

"I don't know. I'm just really not feeling good."

"You got a headache?"

"No . . . I don't know. I really don't feel good."

She sat up in bed. He turned on the light on his night stand. He looked at her face. She was sweating. She really didn't look all too good.

"What is it?"

"I don't know. I really have no idea."

"Are you going to be sick?"

"I don't know."

"Is it serious?"

"I think I should go get checked out or something."

"Checked out? You mean go to the hospital? Right now? What is it?"

"I don't know." She struggled to stand up. He stood up too.

"I'll take you. Let me wake up Isis and we'll all go."

"No, it's OK. Stay here. I can drive myself."

"Are you serious? Don't be crazy. Let me go wake up Isis."

"Elmer, please. You gotta wake up early and if we wake Isis up it'll take forever to get her back to sleep. I can drive myself. Please, papa, just go back to sleep. I'm sure it's not even anything that serious. Go back to sleep and I'll be here when you wake up in the morning, OK?"

He gave in. He got back in bed and she put on some sweatpants and a hoodie and left and he fell asleep almost immediately.

■

The phone was ringing. He looked at the clock. It glowed 11:47 p.m.

He picked up the phone.

"Hello?"

"Is Elmer Vasquez there?"

His forehead almost instantly had a sheen of sweat on it. "Yes he is. Who is this?"

"This is Dr. Bodine at the Denbigh Hospital. You need to get here immediately, sir. Your wife is in labor."

.

He sat in a waiting room staring at a wall, Isis on his lap asleep against his chest. So far he'd spoken to a couple of nurses. No one knew anything. No one could give him a straight answer. All they knew was the room number she was in and that the doctor would come by eventually to speak to him.

Hospitals, the DMV, the post office, airports, the Greyhound station, jail. They all felt the same. It was all some sick waiting game, waiting to hear from some son of a bitch who felt superior, who somehow held your fate in their hands, who knew they had the control because they had the answer you'd sit there and wait for until they knew you were right about to crack. Sometimes they'd even wait until the moment you did crack, because when you cracked you didn't care anymore, the anger blew out of you like a powerful groaning wind, and you could accept any news because nothing mattered anymore, your sanity was used up for those twenty-four hours.

A tall man with glasses in a white coat came up to him. He was bald on the top of his head and looked at Elmer down over his glasses.

"Did you know your wife was pregnant, sir?"

"No. I had no idea."

"She claims she had no idea either. It's pretty incredible, but, as rare as it is, these things do happen."

The doctor kept talking, trying to explain. Elmer barely listened. Another kid. Where in the hell. Another kid. Another kid, was all he could think. Another kid. Two kids. Working for Buster wasn't going to cut it anymore. It just wasn't going to be enough. He could already tell that.

"Would you like to see your child, Mr. Vasquez?"

Elmer nodded and followed the doctor into the next room, Isis in his arms. Esperanza was laying on a bed. She looked like a mess, but strangely enough, there was some kind of contentment in her face as he walked in. Her hair was spread on the pillow, on her forehead. She was holding their newborn. She looked up at him weakly. She waited to see what his reaction would be.

He put Isis down and walked closer.

"You had a baby," he said.

"I know."

"I should've drove you."

"It's OK. I made it."

Elmer felt like he was going to start crying. Whenever his face got that way, she always wound up crying first. "Do you want to hold him?" she asked.

"It's a boy?"

"Yes," she answered.

"OK."

She lifted him slowly and he took him in his arms. He was so pale. He was so little. He was even smaller than Isis when she'd been born, much smaller. He felt like his legs might give, but he held up.

"Congratulations, Mr. Vasquez," the doctor said from behind him.

Elmer didn't say anything. He just cradled his tiny son, staring head-on into the rest of his life. He could see his house and the grass in the yard in the morning and the traffic on the way to work and the inside of his head where no music played, just thousands, millions, of thoughts and ideas and hopes that would all disappear when he stepped out of his truck.

GEMS SCRAPING THE EDGE

The curtain came apart and the chef came out and pointed at him.

"Service," he said.

Fenton stepped into the kitchen and the sound and heat and smell of the place hit him all at once. A goblin woman looked up at him as she scrubbed a mountain of plates, her eyes insane and frantic. The chef's back was to him and when he turned to face Fenton his forehead was beaded with sweat and he had a plate in each hand. He thrust them forth and licked his lips and said, "Table 26."

"Table 26," Fenton repeated robotically, and left that hellish world behind the curtain.

Fenton arrived at the aforementioned table and laid down one dish before a woman and the other in front of a man and said, "Shrimp and grits."

The man looked down at the dish and then his head jerked up at Fenton as if the not-so-distant date of his death had been laid before him, and said simply, "No."

"No? You didn't order the shrimp and grits?"

"Yes," he said then.

Fenton stared at him a moment longer and turned away before all kindness and courtesy left him, vanishing amongst the chaos of the swarming restaurant to leave the man with whatever he wanted to believe was true.

Across the dining room, the crash of wine glasses and champagne flutes shattering everywhere. A girl stood there, giggling stupidly, red faced, unable to draw any other expression but the acceptance of her own ineptitude.

An older gentleman smiled and shrugged. He must have thought she was cute.

■

It was over. The staff, mostly made of the kitchen, stood in the back around a table and in the center of the table was a bottle of Jameson and a stack of plastic cups and the chef poured the Irish whiskey into each cup and they held them up and took them down and some of them coughed and others closed their eyes. Fenton threw his cup away and said goodnight and left.

He rode his bike home the same way every night. The trees hung low and cast shadows. Streetlights seemed menacing. But there was an old cop with a thick mustache in front of a building Fenton passed, every night. And every night as Fenton passed him, the old cop nodded his head and waved. And Fenton would wave back. He liked that old cop.

He rode his bike up to an intersection. He heard something and braked. Out of the darkness, a black horse came plodding down the street. Even in the night, its black mane seemed to shimmer with a terrible majesty. Atop the horse, rode a man wearing a helmet, visor down. He stared at Fenton a moment and a moment only and then they passed, as if the two had simply been some dreadful hallucination come in and out of his delirium.

Real or not, he rode his bike the rest of the way home bent forward like a gargoyle, pedaling like a mother.

Fenton unlocked both sets on the door and stepped inside and locked the door behind him. He turned on the light and took off his shirt and jeans and shoes and socks and sat down. He turned on some music from his laptop and closed his eyes. He let the relief seep into his bones. He wished he could fall asleep, just like that. But that was impossible. The adrenaline never leaves your body that quickly, no matter the hours you've invested. Not even when you believe with all your heart you have absolutely nothing else to give. There's always more to scrape from inside the barrel.

So he took out his phone and texted her.

He stared at the phone a moment after, foolishly expecting it to light up instantly with her response. He put the phone down and peeled himself out of the chair and went to the refrigerator. Nothing but a six pack of PBR, some tortillas, and spicy mustard. Fenton took one of the PBRs.

He drank beer and listened to music for a couple hours. He wondered where she was. What she could be doing. He wondered what movie his neighbor was watching. He went through all six beers. When he was done, he took a piss and brushed his teeth and looked in the mirror for a long time. Then he turned off the lights and got into bed as if it were a coffin.

Fenton closed his eyes and at that very moment his phone began to vibrate. He reached in the dark for it and looked at the screen.

It was her. The text stated nothing other than an address. He laid back in bed and closed his eyes.

Then he got out of bed and turned on the lights.

∎

He was riding his bike in the dark again and the fear from before had been substituted with something else. A kind of wonder. An excitement.

He rode fast, headphones blaring. Beads of every color hung from telephone wires and the gates of people's houses. He rode fast but always kept his eyes on the road. The city was old. The streets were treacherous and perpetually broke—giant potholes like gaping maws, sudden trolley tracks only half buried, street beneath street, gravel like quicksand. This was exciting too. This was the arduous path. And she would be there, standing at the end.

But when he rode over the train tracks, some measure of reality settled back into his secret thoughts. This effect always occurred, whenever Fenton rode over train tracks, anywhere. He didn't know at what age it had started happening, if it was because of watching too many movies or reading too many books. Whatever fantasy he'd grafted into the current affair, train tracks always, always stood for caution. A border was being crossed here and comforts from one place did not necessarily carry into the next.

Finally, there was the address, hovering right above the red door. He'd arrived.

Fenton nodded at a man with a green mohawk, sitting on the porch, legs dangling, and went inside the building.

Light wasn't for this place. Walls had been knocked out and ascents had been crudely constructed to take one to a second floor where people peered down like spying children through holes where living rooms should've been. A built-in cave with slumming bohemians fooling with gadgetry and wires, rasps of guitars and sound checks, a sparse crowd already beginning to form, hungry for any distraction. A couch made out of tires already occupied by lounging sirens with bored expressions, so old already in the blossom of their youth, all but for their glowing skin, as if summer were here. Fenton was wearing his jean jacket.

He turned to a black woman with milk cloud eyes who smiled

when his gaze came upon her and she asked with soothing voice, "Drink?"

He asked for a beer and whiskey and read the scribbled price from off a piece of cardboard. Fenton gave her the money and she felt it and smiled and handed him the drinks. He said thank you and turned away.

Fenton passed all the people inside and went into the back of the building. Water streamed into a pool dug into the floor, full of lily pads and tiny darting fish, orange, black, and white. He sat down next to it and drank his beer. He listened to the water whisper.

This little sanctuary. He could have biked back home after a handful of minutes sitting there like that, floating in nostalgia and serenity, and been satisfied. Gone to sleep. Work the next inevitable and brutal double. And then she appeared, conjured in spite of his peaceful resolution.

"How we doing, Buddha?"

He turned around. She already had a beer in her hand. She was really a sight.

It was a shimmering green dress with feathers of every color everywhere. Crazy makeup and gold glitter. Her blond hair seemed to meld seamlessly with the crown she'd made for herself, this self-styled queen of pigeons. She held up her arms and the feathers hung as if they really were wings and she turned her head, closing her eyes and smiling. Fenton clapped.

"Amazing. Amazing," he said.

She helped him up. He stared at her in awe.

"It was a big party and everyone was dressed up but then it just got stale and, well, it was time to leave. I like your jean jacket," she laughed.

"Thanks."

"I'm glad you came," she said sincerely.

"Well," he said, looking down, "I'm glad too."

They stood there, smiling, silent, the universe on the verge of collapse.

"Have you been out back yet?"

Fenton shook his head.

"Come on."

He followed her outside and up spiral stairs that went up into a night become cool. A bonfire licked upwards in the expanse of the yard where someone played a ghostly banjo and girls hula-hooped. He stepped over some sleeping body and walked across a net of rope suspended in the air, looking down, already too late to second guess. The way she pressed on so resolutely canceled the existence of concepts like alarm and doubt.

A group of vagrants sat on a platform there in the sky passing around a joint. They joined them as if they were old friends. The stars looked wonderful.

The joint came to him and he didn't ask. It hit powerfully.

"Take your time," someone said.

An older man next to him was looking into the sky. There a plane blinked down at them but they couldn't hear it.

"Cadillacs swimming in a dead static TV sky," the man said. "And us. Gems scraping the edge. All of us."

Fenton looked at him and didn't stop until he caught himself drooling. Embarrassed, he wiped his mouth. He hadn't realized the whole of himself was being sucked into that old man's soul. As if he was just breathing Fenton in. He moved away from the man but the man looked back at him with no malice and Fenton knew he had to be more careful with his love. He remembered the railroad tracks. He was out of the man's spell then, but when he looked around the party, she was no longer among them.

There was nowhere to go but onward. But he was alone.

He thought about leaving right then. Something told him tonight was not yet over.

He stepped past the group, apologizing, holding onto the netting, for the first time realizing how high up in the air they were, his overflowing confidence cut in half with her disappeared somewhere. Could he even find her? Fenton had no idea where the fuck he was himself. I'm going to fall and splatter my brains, he thought. Fenton pushed that out of his head. No rearview mirrors, he made that his new mantra. No rearview mirrors.

He climbed a ladder into some bunker. The place was candlelit. She sat on the ground Indian-style with some other guy. She looked at him and smiled.

"Hey," Fenton said.

She stood up and took his hand. They went back down, but down a different ladder, or it seemed like it. But he'd found her. He wasn't alone.

They were walking through some other spider web tunnel and Fenton stopped and said, "What are we doing here?"

"Let's go swimming."

"What just happened up there?" he asked her.

"I'm a bumblebee," she told him.

"What?"

"He told me. My spirit animal is a bumblebee. Do you know what yours is?"

Fenton looked up into the sky. There was the moon, big as hell. He resisted the urge.

"Where are we going?"

"We're going swimming."

"Now?"

"Now."

They returned to the earth from the maze in the sky and ran through the cracked-open house, past blaring sound and bouncing bodies and guilty light. The green mohawk still out there, smoking a cigarette, nodding, ever watchful, days and storms passing by, nails turning yellow, and there would always be others.

She jumped into a four-door wagon type car.

"My bike," Fenton said.

"Put it in the back," someone yelled.

He got his bike and lifted the hatch and angled it inside. Then he got in the back seat with her. The car started but Fenton felt off suddenly, like he could feel the illusion beginning to dissipate. Something inside him was beginning to feel abrasive and raw. Then he saw a bear was driving.

Or it was someone in a bear costume.

"You ever seen that movie *Finding Nemo*?"

The bear turned to look at Fenton when he said this.

"Yeah."

"This is the part where Nemo rides with the turtles. Except I'm a bear. Well, actually my name's Todd."

Someone handed something back to her and she handed one to Fenton.

"I have to work a double tomorrow," he said.

"Then you probably shouldn't," she said.

He looked up and the bear was looking at him. The bear had a smile on his face. His eyes were so huge.

Fenton took the pill.

She laughed, holding her hand in front of her mouth. Her head went all the way back when she laughed. It was a good thing to watch. He wanted to strangle her neck. Out of a type of love. Ha ha.

They crossed more train tracks.

They played the music so loud. Fenton could feel the bear looking at him from the rearview. He didn't know whether it was out of judgment or that he may have been happy for them. Fenton didn't care. He couldn't keep his hands off of her. Her breath was some maddening mix of menthol cigarettes and huckleberry. Her neck was a pillow that turned into a bed that turned into a dream.

Air rushing by, bass pulsing from every side, each crack and crater in the road like a spaceship kissing an asteroid. Everything inside of him seemed to be feeling the world for the first time. And it was nowhere near the first time, but what no one told you was there many, many worlds, and you have the chance to live in several. Maybe not always or all the time, only on nights like this, days or mornings like this, fleeting, like a song you never hear again but forever recall the melody. He put his arm out the window and watched it turn into a snake slithering up into the black universe. Like he had a place to go. Like home was out there somewhere.

No. Then he knew for sure, none of it was true. There wasn't a way he or anybody could know that was true.

They got out of the car like zombies and followed the bear and Fenton realized there were more than the two of them and that bear. They went through a gate and he could hear it. Lights came on. A pool. Someone ran straight for it. Even just the sound of a splash time-shifted every single one of them to childhood.

■

Fenton was doing a Spider-Man crawl on the walls of the pool because he hadn't yet learned how to swim. It was his aunt's pool and he was in love with her.

She was so beautiful. Except she wasn't his aunt. She just liked him to call her that. She had big fluffy hair like a cloud had attached itself to her head, and the cloud was black, but for the first time not in any type of ominous way. She wore big dark sunglasses. He knew the eyes behind those sunglasses held nothing but love for him.

When she smiled, with those red lips, Fenton wished he could grow years in seconds so that in hours she'd let him kiss her.

He remembered that as they'd had arrived, the man Fenton's mother said was his aunt's boyfriend was leaving. He left on a motorcycle. He was wearing a black helmet. Fenton never saw his face. The visor was down. Fenton hated him. He knew the man couldn't be good for her. But there's no way to articulate those types of feelings when you are a child. Not without bursting.

Everyone left the pool to go inside to eat. Fenton stayed out there, holding onto the wall and letting his legs float in the water. He was flying somewhere. These were his earliest memories of solitary wanderlust. These things stay with you for the rest of your life.

He let loose the wall and then he drifted too far. He was adrift. But he hadn't yet learned how to swim.

He started to drown. It was the most desperate, loneliest feeling. He was submerged. Light twinkled from above. He could hear people yelling. Someone splashed into the water. His brother saved his life that day. Fenton cried so hard into his arms. They all held him.

■

Fenton was being pulled back up and was lifted out of the water and laid down. When he opened his eyes, dazed, just above him was the bear. Todd. Those big eyes and his indestructible smile. I will trust you forever.

The sun was coming up.

"I have to go to work," Fenton told the bear, still looking up at him.

"Let me take you home," Todd said.

And he did. The bear dropped him off. Awkwardly, Fenton hugged him. His wet, bear arms wrapped around him.

"Thank you," Fenton told him.

"Have a good day at work," Todd the bear said. He lingered a moment as Fenton removed his bike from the back, and then drove off.

Fenton went inside his apartment and brushed his teeth. He had ten minutes to get to work.

He was ten minutes late.

He locked up his bike and as he did he felt his phone vibrate in his pocket. He took it out and read the message.

Good luck today, she'd sent.

He smiled, even though it hurt to.

He came in through the back gate. His manager sat there, smoking a cigarette. He looked up at Fenton from his glasses.

"You're late," he said. "Did you go for it last night?"

"I did."

"Did you get it?" he asked.

"I don't know."

He stood up and came up very close to Fenton. His manager had always seemed a diminutive character since his employment at the restaurant but at that moment he seemed to loom over him.

"Nothing you do is new," he said.

Those words seemed to pound on top of Fenton like a *Super Mario* mallet.

"Go inside and get dressed and get ready for work. Get your shit together. Because we're gonna get fucked today."

And they did. Get fucked. But they made it through. As you always do, one way or another. Whether it ends in victory, inconsequence, or misery. You always make it through. Until, finally, you find a way out. And then your days will never be like these. And that's another thing you have to prepare for, or settle for, or be grateful for. More train tracks. More swimming pools. And if you're lucky, you may be granted a guardian angel that saves you from the lure of shipwreck, however lovely she may look that night.

FINE QUALITY

One fine day in Brooklyn, I was sitting outside of a restaurant with a new friend. We were waiting on a group of our friends to join us. It was a very nice day, a sunny day, and I was whistling.

A woman came out from the restaurant, I think she was the host. She was very beautiful.

She asked, "Was that you whistling?"

"Yes," I said.

"That was some beautiful whistling."

"Thank you," I told her.

She went back into the restaurant. I looked at my friend and he was smiling really big. That made me smile, like a little boy's smile. My new friend was happy for me. I knew we could become good friends. It's a fine quality when your friends can be happy for you when the good things happen.

I WALKED WITH A ZOMBIE

There was a band playing in the bar we were at, this honky-tonk bar, and people were dancing. Rooster was out there with his girl, twirling her around, and they looked great, and the band sounded great. I sat at the table alone drinking a Lone Star, tapping my foot, watching everyone dance.

When the song finished, Rooster and his girl came back over to the table. Rooster came back looking very serious, like he always looked when he knew he'd just finished doing a good job at something. They both sat down and reached for their drinks.

"Y'all looked great," I said.

His girl smiled at me and Rooster said, "Let's take a shot."

I said, "OK."

"That OK, honey?" Rooster asked his girl politely.

She said it was and we stood up as if we had some chore to finish and walked to the bar. I put my elbow on the counter and a girl came over and I ordered two shots of Bulleit. She put two shot glasses on the counter and filled them up and I put cash on the wood and handed a glass to Rooster and took one myself. We cheersed and put it down and smacked the glasses back on the counter.

"You gonna go out there and dance? Lot of cute girls here," Rooster said.

"Nah. Ain't feeling it tonight."

"How come?"

"Just ain't."

We walked back to the table and sat down. I looked back out on the dance floor. All the girls wore floral dresses and cowboy boots and the boys wore their shirts tucked and their jeans skinny. Everyone looked young. That was inside. Right outside the bar, in the small lot designated for the smokers and storytellers and wallflowers, it was as if there was a different dress code. Trendier. It was supposed to seem as if there was very little care put to the appearance when in fact it was the opposite. And then just on the other side of the highway, it was vastly different again. More pastel colors. More hair gel. More high heels. More money. It's how it would always be. And still, it sometimes seemed as if it weren't diverse enough. Texas was very different from the east coast.

I guess I missed home.

"Do you wanna go to another bar?" I asked.

Rooster looked at his girl and she looked back at him. Then he looked at me and said, "I think we're probably gonna head out."

"OK."

"You gonna stay out?"

"Probably."

"You gonna go to another bar?"

"I think so."

"You oughta dance with some girl here."

"Nah."

"You want us to give you a ride somewhere?"

"Nah. I feel like walking tonight."

We finished our drinks and stood up. The band had just started a slow song. Couples filled the dance floor.

"We're gonna dance to this one real quick," Rooster said.

"OK," I said, "I'll see you, bud."

"Be safe tonight."

"I will."

We hugged and then I hugged his girl and gave her a kiss on the cheek. I turned and walked towards the door. When I got there the doorman opened the door for me and I looked back a final time to the dance floor and they were already out there, arms around each other, swaying. I walked out.

I stuck my hands in my pockets and cut out of the parking lot and headed down the street, turning at the corner. Ahead of me was an intersection. I came up to it and stopped. The light was red. Across the street, I could see a girl coming towards me and the intersection. She was by herself. She had blond hair. I could see she had wide hips. She kept right on walking through the intersection, no regard for the light.

I was watching her and didn't seem to notice anything else and she took those few steps into the street and before someone could snap their fingers, there was a car and the sound and my own exclamation bursting forth. The car picked her up and she rolled over the hood and the length of the car like some life-size rag doll and then just dropped back onto the street with a terrible thud and she lay there.

The car's brake lights glowed red and the car shuddered and began to zigzag and then, as if it were some gigantic and oblivious fly that had smacked into a window, drove on and did not turn back.

My first instinct was to chase the car. Half a second later, I realized that was stupid and ran to the girl instead. I had an awful knot-twist in my stomach. An instant sheen of sweat on my forehead. I got to her and dropped to my knees and put my hands on her. She almost immediately moved to my touch, not fully turning, but as if someone had awoken her. Very slowly, she turned her head up and looked at me. She had brown eyes and freckles that ran across her nose and onto her cheeks.

"Are you OK?" I asked. I looked around to see if I'd been the only one to witness the whole thing. No one was around. I was the only one.

She didn't answer me. She looked around and then sat up, not saying a word, just observing the world around her as if she'd taken a nap as natural as could be, right there in the middle of the street.

She had plenty of scratches all over and a good nick under her eye, but nothing seemed serious. She'd have to get some water on a knee and her elbows. I wanted to pick the tiny rocks out, but it seemed a tad too intimate a task for a stranger. I asked her again.

"Hey. Are you OK? Jesus, you just got hit by a car. They just ran off. I wanted to chase them."

She started to try to stand up. I helped her. She wobbled only a second, then she seemed fine. I held on to her a couple moments longer.

"Should I call 911?" I asked her.

"God," she said. "I was going to have a beer."

"Well. So was I. You got hit by a car," I said, as if I'd been the only one to notice.

"I feel like I got the air sucked out of me." She looked around. I noticed I was still holding her arm. I let go and when I did she looked at me. "Jeez," she said.

"Are you really OK? You're cut up but . . . you're not bleeding much. It's a miracle."

"I was going to have a beer," she repeated.

"Well. If you really think you're all right to."

A bar wasn't far off. This part of town, one never was. There wasn't any dancing in this one and the jukebox played no music. We got some beers and sat in our stools and I watched her the whole time, still amazed. It was as if she'd only tripped and fell and scraped herself up. But she was well enough to drink and she did as fast as I did and didn't say no to a shot of whiskey.

"You'll want to wash out the dirt from your knee there. Elbows too."

She nodded and drank some more. She watched the television on mute languidly, her head tilted up, occasionally shaking her blond hair from her eyes.

"Were you going to meet some friends?" I asked her.

"I just wanted to get a beer. Crappy night at work. I just had a hankering."

"I understand the feeling. Guess it's that kind of night."

But then it was a last call, and everyone was being ushered to the front to figure things out.

"I don't think I want to go home just yet," she said, still watching the television above the bottles of liquor behind the bar.

"You don't think it might be smart to lay down after all that?" I asked her.

She shrugged, as if what had happened less than an hour ago had been years back.

"I got some beer at my place," I offered.

She looked at me suspiciously a moment, and that made me shrug next. "Unless you got a better idea. I just thought I'd mention it. You know, if that were even an option."

She pursed her lips and then took her beer bottle to her lips and tipped it back until it was finished. She smacked her lips afterwards and asked, "How far away do you live?"

"Just some blocks."

We hardly said a word on the walk there. It wasn't a kind of quiet that scared me. Maybe it should have. The night itself was near all the way silent, with just the sound of moving vehicles far off in the distance where the highways were and the sound of cicadas up in the trees, as normal as air conditioners. In a few days, the moon would be full. The moon always looked great in the big Texas sky. There was no breeze. I could smell the trees. To the west, you could see all the buildings downtown glowing. It was just warm enough to feel my shirt stick to my chest.

We went on slowly, but I didn't mind. I still hardly had a gauge on whether she was really OK or not, but I didn't want to keep asking. It irritated me when people did that. I'd glance over at her and see her next to me with her chin almost cupped into her chest. Her shoulders swayed in the smallest way with every step. Her hair seemed more blond, her skin becoming duskier with only the light from the streetlamps. I wanted to say something or touch her, just to have her look up, so I could see her face and have an idea of what she was thinking, but I was too scared it would change her mind.

Nothing passed us on the way there either. That should've seemed strange. It should've also seemed strange, I knew, that neither of us were still not saying anything. She'd just rolled over a car, I had to keep reminding myself. But I thought about that less and less. I finally decided to just go along. It didn't feel like tonight was a thing where hard decisions had to be made. The door would open and you walked through it or you didn't. In truth, I loved these kinds of nights.

"What's your name?" I asked her. It didn't really matter but I wanted to hear her talk again.

"Renee," she said. She didn't ask me what my name was.

Coming up to my apartment complex, a cat sat in front of us on the sidewalk. As we came up it arched its back and hissed at us, then ran away.

I kicked the air for effect. "I hate cats," I said. "Well, not actually. I'm just allergic to them. I guess I've never had the chance to see if we'd get along or not."

We came up to my door. I took out my keys and unlocked it and we walked in. You could smell dog in the place. I turned on the lights and we walked into my kitchen. I opened the fridge and took out two beers and we went into the living room and sat on the couch. I opened the beers and handed one to her.

"You got any roommates?" she asked me.

"A roommate and a dog."

"He here?"

"Yup. Upstairs. Asleep. He works in the day."

She sat back in the couch and closed her eyes. I examined the nick under her eye again and could tell it would be blue tomorrow. Now I could see besides the scratches her shirt was torn a little and her shorts were smudged with black. She opened her brown eyes again and looked at me and it made me a little nervous with how she looked at me.

"I oughta clean those scratches for you." I made to get up.

"In a minute. Sit here a while." She drank her beer. "I had a hell of a day," she said.

"I'm glad you can still walk around. I'm glad I met you, even under the crazy circumstances."

She leaned forward and I understood that, and we kissed. Her lips were cold. I touched her hair. I'd been wanting to the whole night.

She broke the kiss and clawed my face.

"What the fuck?" I almost yelled.

She looked surprised. She didn't say anything.

"Why did you do that?" I said, holding my jaw, more from alarm than pain.

"I'm sorry," she said, her mouth open, like she didn't believe she'd done it. Or that I was having the reaction I was having. I couldn't tell which.

"What the hell?" I said.

"Please," she said, softer than anything else she'd said that night. She bowed her head so that her forehead came up to my lips. I hesitated, then I put my arms around her. We sat there quiet for a long time, on the couch, me just holding her like that for a while, my lips on her forehead. Then her cheek. Her neck. And back to her cold lips. Finally, we stood up and went to my bedroom.

■

I woke up. It was still dark outside. A very low blue light came through the blinds. I was alone in the bed. I sat up quickly. Renee was sitting in the chair next to my desk, with her knees up, staring at me.

"Renee," I said.

I couldn't tell a thing from her face. Her expression was completely blank and I couldn't tell if it was a vague contempt behind her eyes or if she was as dazed as she was when I'd rushed up to her on the street. She sat there, arms around her knees, like she was just a picture of something, staring from a frame, staring at some photographer I didn't know.

"Hey. You OK?" I asked her. I sat on the edge of the bed, closer to her, close enough to reach her, and I touched her leg.

"I couldn't sleep," she said. She sounded like the saddest person in the world when she said that. It ran a shock through me.

"Come back to bed."

She stood up slowly and came into the bed and I held her

underneath the blankets and she was cold in my arms but I held her there and it wasn't long until I was asleep again.

■

It was the sun coming through the blinds this time, and grackles instead of cicadas, and I woke up and I was alone. I sat up from my bed. Renee was gone.

I got up and went to the bathroom first. I had two glasses of water to get the ash of last night out of my mouth. I went to the bedroom and looked for a note or anything. Nothing. Even just a number and I wouldn't have instantly felt that pit in my gut.

I walked back out into the living room. Two half-drunk bottles of beer still sat on the coffee table. I put a hand to my jaw. There was dried blood there.

WHERE POP GREW UP

My dad picked me up off of South Street, right before the South Street Bridge that took you over to West Philly. He had his big truck with him, and he must've just taken it to the wash because it looked like a commercial. The sun caught it when he pulled up. This silver chariot. I waved at him from the stoop I was sitting on, stood up, skipped down the steps and hopped up into the truck.

"Damn, boy," my dad said. "Looking scruffy." He laughed.

I rubbed my chin. "Was a long weekend, Pop."

Dad laughed again. "It's Wednesday."

We started driving. He had his window down. The wind that came in was cold, but I didn't complain. I just put my hands in the pockets of my coat and drew it in closer. We were headed north.

"How you been, Pop?" I asked my dad.

"Oh, you know," he said, letting the wind snatch up the ash from his Camel.

Personally, I thought Philadelphia was a beautiful place. But I had to confess something too. I needed light as much as I needed darkness. So on days like this, where the sky was somewhere in between heaven and hell, and the clouds were up there lingering, loitering, maybe even with a dour demeanor, it didn't threaten my fate, because I needed days like this, even looked forward to them. Explain that to somebody. You'd be surprised at who gets it.

The people indigenous to this city were maybe like that in a way. I won't tell you there aren't any pretenders. Pretenders are unavoidable in life, at the basest levels of nature and its highest echelons both. But not everywhere was authenticity valued. I wasn't sure where that originated from. Because sometimes it felt bitter, and sometimes it felt like pure joy. So maybe . . . that was the whole point.

"So?" my dad said. "Tell me what's going on up here. You need money?"

"Nah, I don't need money," I said, a little irritated. But I dismissed the feeling quickly, because I could recall so many times I had needed it. And that my father was not asking to be an asshole, but because he wanted to get it out of the way so we wouldn't have to hedge other topics of conversation. I got to act annoyed, indignant, but we both felt the relief of that issue passing us, knowing it didn't have to be a source of tension held between the two of us. The ride felt lighter immediately.

"Well, you hungry?" he asked me.

"Sure. OK," I answered.

■

I was a little boy, barely beginning any kind of school, and my shorts went high up my brown thighs and my socks went up to my calves and my hair was grown out, like a kind of curly dark halo. I was on the sidewalk in front of my father's family home, the one he'd grown up in, North Philly. I was playing with the pigeons, feeding them pieces of bread. I was having a ball.

All the different kinds. There weren't just grey ones. There were white ones, with brown rings around their eyes. Brown ones, with white wings. Black ones with white bellies and green throats. Beautiful automobiles glided by, shining. Everyone's yards, the bushes were cut and trimmed meticulously, stoops swept immaculately, and every hour, the ice cream man serenaded his way down the street like the fiddler on the roof.

"You know them pigeons just be rats with wings, right?"

I looked up, squinting. It was my uncle Chip. He was grinning at me, with his Tic Tac-white teeth, and a cigarette hanging magically from his lip. I stood up and hugged his waist.

We walked up into the house of my grandparents. The porch had a screen barrier all around it. On the couch was my pop-pop and his son, my father, smoking more cigarettes. They looked at me like they could comprehend the bucket of trouble I was.

"Time to eat!" my grandma called from inside. She sounded like she was deep inside of some cave. I could see figures past the screen door, shadows shuffling, preparing the dinner table for a feast. And wasn't food always the way good people congregated to share their love?

I will admit, I was scared of my great grandmother. When humans get that damn old, as a child, you can't help but feel they are aliens. I can't remember her eyes at all. Just the huge glasses, her fake teeth, the whiskers on her chin.

I don't remember the food like I know it now. I remember the food like the first girl you ever had a crush on. Like the first time you ever went to the beach. Like the first time you wake up with your pet dog next to you, still peaceful and adorable in slumber. Nostalgia is a trap.

I never really remembered my mother in those moments. Which is crazy to think now. To think, now, in my life. How bigger than life she'd always been, but back then, quiet, submissive, pretty, wavy black hair, not in the company of the men, who sat separately with their cigarettes discussing things far outside my realm of understanding.

And when it was over, and I could be left to my own devices once again, I was back on the sidewalk, back with the pigeons. I don't know why. I'm an adult now. I hate pigeons. As an adult, I regard them as rats with wings.

■

We were driving into North Philly. Dad had finished the cigarette and had the window back up.

"Dang, it's been forever huh, Pop?"

"Yeah," he said.

I can't remember exactly when we'd stopped coming back. At some point, his parents died. Pop-Pop. Mom-Mom. I was at the funeral, and then that was it. No more. I don't remember if I asked, but I didn't even know if there was anyone to come back to. Seems like a crazy thing to lose track of. Your family. I was only in my late twenties. I already wasn't talking to my younger brothers. Rarely ever with my sister. And my parents? My dad wasn't unfair to ask about money. The chances weren't bad that I was asking for it. But right then, I was good. So I could be proud of that. As fleeting as it was. Goddamn. It's a trip to go through life, going back and forth from being poor to having money, poor to having money, poor to having money. Tell me how I still had good credit. Tell me that then.

I crunched up the wrapper to my steak sandwich and put it in the side compartment. I licked my fingertips. Then I put my hands back into my pockets. The scenery grew more desolate. More boarded up houses. Litter everywhere, like unnatural tumbleweeds, rolling down the gutters. There were the real weeds too. I actually welcomed the sight of them. Something true come from the earth, even if they had no admirers. Cars abandoned, wheels missing, other parts too. They were now street sculptures. And scattered, there were corners occupied with men probably my dad's age but appearing even older, standing there staring suspiciously, even though it was just early afternoon on a weekday. Standing out there in their coats and jackets and scarves and hats, smoking cigarettes, looking and looking, because after all, this was still theirs. Their home, their territory. No. It wasn't ever theirs. But neither had it been taken from them. They'd been pushed out here, far away from where anyone would see them. Except those who might return home.

"Still there, I see," my dad clucked, as if addressing my thoughts.

"Huh?" I said back, emerging from my reverie.

"That warehouse there," he pointed, his eyeballs just over his rimless glasses. "Used to work there, packing. Only took 'em six months before they made me manager. Had keys to the whole place. Pop-Pop couldn't believe it. One night, I brought all my buddies over there. After the shift. Whole place was shut down. Dark. We had a bunch of beer. Got drunk as hell. Drank all night in there. I remember. Lights shined in, thought it was the cops. We were ready to peel out. Every man for himself. It was just your Uncle Chip. Getting off late. We just kept drinking."

He laughed a little bit. He slapped the wheel. Then he stopped. His face became very serious. I didn't ask him why. It wasn't my place. I craned my neck back to look at that warehouse, the windows blown out, the roof gone, the inside looking like an empty cold oven with only crumbs left behind. We moved on.

Dad parked his big shiny truck in front of the house. The old house, where he'd grown up, where I'd visited so many summers of my childhood. It had been chipping green paint back then and the green was all but gone now to leave behind a sick grey color.

The entire block looked like a ghost town. Almost every house boarded up. Less than three cars parked on the block. The bodega I used to go to buy lollipops and pork rinds from, when I was that little boy, big hair, baby thighs, that bodega was no more.

And the house my father grew up in. The screened-in porch was dark, the screen itself cut up, crudely, meanly. Just beyond it, the doors to the actual house, also boarded up, like all the rest. No one lived here anymore.

"Did you know?" I asked.

"Knew someone else had bought it. Didn't know anything after," my dad told me, staring.

He stood there, both hands on his hips. He was wearing a suede jacket. He had a sharp haircut. I realized he'd made himself look good for this. Just in case. He almost looked young again. I remembered how handsome my father used to be, back then. Hell, he was still handsome. This son of a bitch still tucked his shirt into his jeans.

"Well, well, well," an old gravelly voice said from some unseen place. "Look at this. That you, Slim? Back after all this time?"

I looked around, everywhere, trying to see who was talking. My dad must've already known. He didn't grin or laugh or anything. Stood right there, hands on his hips like he had been. Just a little curve to his lips, like he knew the answer to a trick question.

"Yeah. It's me, Whit. You still out here, huh?" my dad asked.

"Ain't dead yet," the deep voice said.

"Nope. Not yet."

"Come on up. You and your boy. Look at him. He grown too, huh."

"Nah," my dad said. "He just think he is."

I remembered Whit. The next door neighbor. He was old even back even. He wore his hair in dreads and always wore sunglasses, even if he was in doors. He had them on still. And his voice sounded like it was coming from the inside of an old chimney.

We three sat on the porch, the two of them smoking cigarettes. My dad took a drag off his and looked at me, not specifically, but more like noticing I was alive and present. It's hard to express how rare that sensation can feel. Sometimes it's all a person wants. He took his pack of smokes out of the breast pocket of his jacket and pulled back the top and offered it to me. He'd never once in his life done this before. By then, I'd already quit smoking. I reached forward and snagged one anyway. He leaned forward with a rusty golden Zippo and lit it. I leaned forward too, and when I leaned back, I blew a plume of smoke in the air. We all sat quiet, ruminating.

"That your truck?" Whit asked.

"Yup," my dad said.

"Big. Nice. You driving that around here, huh?"

"Just came up to visit my boy," my dad told him.

Whit leaned up, checking me out. "You live here now, huh? Isn't that something. And you ain't even from here. Shiiiit. What part of town you in?"

"Around Center City. On South Street," I answered.

Whit leaned back. "Mmhmm," he murmured knowingly.

"Anybody from back in the day still around?" my dad asked, and his tone struck me, because it sounded lighter than I'd normally recognize. An unexpected hopefulness that perked my ears and made me wonder if it were the same man but from a different time.

"Nah. Everybody gone," Whit told him.

We sat there for the duration of our respective cigarettes in silence, smoking. Old Man Whit had an empty washed out tomato can jar where he threw all his butts in and we honored that.

"This hood's on its way out. I gotta take two bus rides just to do groceries," Whit told us. "But you did all right. Got to see some of the world. You made it out."

"I just did the military. Nothing special," my dad said.

"But you did make it out. Only one thing I ever wonder about. And I guess it makes sense in some ways. I been here long enough. I still can see. I can't see a lot, but I still can see. I wonder why whenever anyone gets out, how come they never come back? How come it can only go the one way? But I get it. Why would you, right? Why come back to this. When you'd do anything to get out. I get it."

My dad sighed. It almost seemed like he saw the question was coming. Anticipated it. A dream he'd already had. He must have. "I never had a chance to get the house back, Whit. They had a lot of debt I didn't know about. I had a family to raise."

"Right. With your overseas wife," Whit said, emphasizing overseas in a way I didn't understand, but knew I shouldn't like. "Funny how the military works. Can't be mad at you though. Wife. Family. That big truck. I ain't mad, Slim."

My dad stood up. "I'm glad you ain't."

The way my dad said that, his voice once again sounded different. Different from how he talked to most people in front of me, actually. It sounded like there was a weight attached that I had never recognized before. Never considered. I wasn't supposed to see my dad like that. Not my dad or mom or older brother or a teacher. This was for private. I sat there, looking at him, feeling like I was all wrong to be there.

"We're gonna walk up the block, then head out. I just wanted to take a look at things one more time. It was good to see you, Whit. You take care of yourself," my dad said.

I stood up too. I was a man by then, but only biologically. In that moment, I felt I should've been crouched on the sidewalk, feeding pigeons.

"I ain't see you at Chip's funeral," Whit said.

We all went still. I slowly looked at my dad. He was staring at the floor.

"No one told me when it was. I didn't find out until after," he said.

"Well," Whit said. "You were missed, Slim. You and your family take care."

My dad stood there a moment, his fists clenched. I dared not look at him straight on, only from the edges of my eye. I could see he was shaking. Just a little bit.

"You take care, Whit," my dad said.

We left the porch, stepping down just several stairs, back onto the sidewalk. We started walking up the block. There was absolutely no one else around. It was so quiet. How it ought to be in nature, but we were deep in the city. And only early afternoon. I'd never been anywhere in my life in the early afternoon where it was this quiet. I hadn't really begun camping yet, I guess. Anyway, I didn't look at my dad, I just asked him.

"You OK?"

"Yeah," he said. "Just wanted to see."

We got to the end of the block. The bodega was boarded up and painted over. I hadn't seen a single pigeon. Even they knew.

"Let's head out. We can go do something fun. You tell me," my dad said, his hand on my shoulder. He had on his sunglasses, so I couldn't see his eyes.

CICI'S CRUSHER

Suzanne and I ushered the children into the Cici's Pizza like we were herding a school of corgis. They rushed all around our legs like wiggly things and we could barely afford to look ahead if we were going to stay upright. But we finally did get to the register and there encountered the fearful eyes of the employees of the restaurant, and they knew as well as Suzanne and I what terrible fate lay in store. I couldn't help but start laughing, and seeing me do so, the kids began to do the same, like the little maniacs that they were. This only increased the panic developing amongst the staff, but there was no going back now.

Suzanne, my partner in this ambitious field trip, was a nice young white lady from Georgia. I always called her Suzanne, never Suzie. I guess we were just older. Our mutual situation didn't seem like the appropriate time to be cute, not with each other anyway. Still, she would learn the kids' new dances in her goofy way, and she could keep her cool as they got rowdy, and she had a fine sense of humor. We got along. I was grateful for her. Grateful to have her help me coral these wild kids and for her calm, because I was still learning it.

It was only my second year of teaching. I was starting to get the hang of it. I took a certain pride in being the only male teacher. The other teachers seemed to like me, and the kids did too, mostly. Almost all the children were black, a few Hispanic, zero white. I think they liked seeing someone who looked like them in me, but that could've been my own separate projection.

I remember my mom's reaction when I told her I was going after this job. She had this funny look on her face. I realized a lot later down the line I'd never had a male teacher around these grades. Not until late middle school actually, or unless it was just gym.

The kids were more than a handful, but I never let myself feel like it was getting over my head. It was almost like I had something to prove really. In my life. I wasn't sure what. I just didn't want to quit. Not this time.

Suzanne was handling payment with the lady behind the counter. She was so good, she could even placate the employees in the face of all the chaos. I looked around, reminiscing about the last time I'd been in this place. Must've been back in college, when I'd come here with the boys. We called those nights "Cici's Crushers." We were monsters, just like these kids, except we were big and we should've known better. We did know better, we just wanted act otherwise. We'd roll in with six or more of us and our sole intention was to eat the restaurant out of pizza. We never did succeed but we gave a valiant effort, and the employees would regard us in awe and disgust and every one of us paid the price that night or the morning next atop the porcelain throne. It was so stupid. But we did stuff like that all the time back then. We went about it with a degree of pride we couldn't explain to anybody, nor ourselves. We didn't really have to, I guess. Looking back, it seemed like a lot of fun, and none of us ever held each other accountable. Goddamn, we were terrible. We loved trouble, celebrated it. I knew I was one of the wildest ones. I also knew that was not something to brag about at all. It had cost me a lot. Now all I had was fun stories, but only if I made it sound like it happened a very, very long time ago. Truthfully, I missed those boys. I told myself, I ought to text them sometime. Say hi. But deep down, I knew I probably wouldn't. I didn't know it up front, but more like a whisper of a thing, way low and hazy, lost in the velvet curtains of a sunny day.

Seemed like Suzanne was finishing up with everything at the counter. The kids had already formed lines with their plates for that pizza buffet to heaven. Someone behind me cooed gently in a thick southern drawl, "Oh, no. No, no, no. Let me get this, y'all."

I turned around to see two men standing there. They both had on camouflage hats and wore button up shirts tucked into their jeans. One of them was growing his hair long and his teeth were spaced out in his mouth as he grinned at us. The other one had porkchop sideburns and a big gut but still wore his shirt tucked in anyway. They were looking directly at me and Suzanne.

"I don't want to have to pay the welfare later on. How's about we just go ahead and pay up front," the one with the teeth said. He pulled out his wallet and took a card out and waved it at us like we were puppies. His buddy started snickering.

Every sound in the place went to mute and all I could hear was my heart hammering right behind my eyeballs. My brain set on fire. An instant ignition. Oh wow, I knew what this was. This feeling. I hadn't felt it in a very long time, but I could recognize it like a song I'd played every night before I went to sleep. I *knew* this feeling. It was like the old days. The bad days that we said were the good days. The days we didn't tell our parents about, the days that made these days the reason none of the boys talked anymore. But then I remembered: Now wasn't the old days. I was far away from that time and that me. So I stood frozen, conflicted. I couldn't move, just felt every muscle inside me screaming at me, and I remembered and I knew what to do. I took a step forward. A robotic step forward. Like I was slowly turning into something else.

A small hand gripped my arm. A tiny hand. I looked down and saw Suzanne's white hand on my black skin, holding me there. I'd always liked Suzanne. Right from the moment I'd met her. You can never really know about people these days, but she seemed like she'd be a nice person, a good teacher, and it just so turned out she was. She looked at me with her pale blue eyes and shook her head and said to the men without taking her eyes away from me, "Thank you, but we got it."

I looked at the men again, with their shitty, trademark, father-passed-to-son smirks, knowing I couldn't do anything, accepting that I couldn't, not here nor in their lives or mine. But I was able to realize that wasn't what was important. I turned away and came up to the counter and got my cup and walked away. I filled the cup with Dr Pepper. Put the plastic lid on and stabbed in the straw. I turned around and saw Suzanne sitting down and staring at me. She was smiling at me, but it was a sad smile, and I knew it was all the rest of the strength she had left to offer, and that it really wasn't much. I felt drained too. So fast, I felt that way. Like someone had just stuck a cord in my back and zapped all the energy out. Funny how many days felt like that lately. And somehow, we'd have to find a way to regain that energy before the kids finished eating. Thank God, they were in full feast mode by then. Having their own little Cici's Crusher. No worries beyond that. No thought to what may lie ahead. Golly. Wasn't that nice. And certainly, for the best. Without question, for the best. Because by now, I knew that sort of bliss would never last.

THE NIGHT I LEARNED
HOW TO TWO-STEP

The tide had broken for a moment at work and I had time to look up and stop using my hands and see who was actually sitting in the restaurant, talking and eating and drinking and laughing. It was a Friday night and it felt like a Friday night. I sighed from deep inside and looked out there, into the dining room. A table caught my eye. A man at the table.

There was about eight of them total, but there was only one black guy. He was sort of in the center and his head was shaved bald and though I couldn't hear him I could see he was speaking very animatedly, very passionately. He seemed upset from the seriousness of his eyebrows. Still, most of the people, particularly the older white men at the table, held expressions of discomfort, indifference, boredom even. The women mostly just looked uncomfortable. A man at the table was looking off, trying to find something to set his attentions to in the restaurant.

I could imagine the conversation. And I knew whatever that man was saying was futile. I could read it all over their faces, each and every one of them. The feigned façade of lame duck outrage. But as soon as the check was paid and they walked back out into the warm night air, they'd be safe again. Safe in their bubble world. They'd feel the relief reenter their fragile bodies. Because once again they wouldn't have to care, or even pretend to care, about anyone other than themselves and the people they kept in their bubble, if they even cared for those people. I felt sorry for the man. Waste of energy, and even more so, you'll be branded after this. I remember a man describing me, once.

"This is Levy. Levy has a lot of opinions."

Old guy. Regular of mine. We got along fine. He probably knew some things I didn't. A lot of things I didn't. But I know I knew some things he didn't either. Still, I picked up what he was putting down. There are just some people you can hear it from and there are some people you'd rather not. Almost as if you are incapable. Your wife, your father, your coworker, your kid. I'm not sure how that develops in the brain, how you can only come to hear truth from a specific person, but I knew I was guilty of it too. We were all guilty, guilty, guilty.

I turned to the other bartender.

"Going offline," I told him. "Take a piss."

"Have fun," she said.

Using one hand to handle my business, I used my other hand to text. I was hitting up Bucket. I said, "Let's learn how to two-step tonight."

"OK," he texted back.

Back then, we were both still kind of new to Austin, and back then, there were still Tejano bars. Don't ask me to name any of them, but I knew where they were. However, their numbers were dwindling rapidly, and we all knew why. Inevitably, there would be none left. It was a sad reality, but the future was coming, and it didn't include the browns nor the blacks. Every night of their numbered existence, you could feel a lot of emotion in those bars. A lot of things people didn't say or found a way to say in some other way.

I was wearing all black, my work uniform, except I'd just thrown a Hawaiian shirt on top. That was how I rolled back then.

Every damn night. I was at the bar drinking a Tecate with hot sauce and salt on the rim. With each Tecate, I had a shot of tequila. Only thing was, I couldn't do rail tequila. I could do rail bourbon because bourbon is bourbon, but tequila isn't something you can fake. I've tried fake tequila. And I won't ever go down that road again.

So that night I was having Espolòn with my Tecate. I was sitting at the bar and Bucket came in. Bucket was tall, and you could smoke in this Tejano bar, so he had a smoke dangling from his lip, and he looked good and so did his hair. He'd started growing it out, which I thought was smart, because when he kept his hair buzzed, it just really seemed like he was being sort of masochistic. Selling himself short. Why cut out one of your greatest powers, right? I know a lot of people do stuff like that. I never understood it, the logic. I don't think they did either. Punishing yourself. For what? Maybe abstain. But don't detract. But that was my opinion. Who am I anyway? I stood up off my stool and we hugged.

There weren't many patrons but the ones there regarded us with a mixture of lazy animosity and languid acceptance. The patrons looked as though they came from another time. Some kind of West World without the white people. Well, except Bucket.

The *caballeros* tucked in their shirts. The *señoras* wore heavy makeup. Everyone combed their hair extravagantly. They spoke softly and laughed loudly. Christmas lights hung on the wall and there was no AC, just fans.

"Not so much a crowd in here," Bucket said, sitting down on the stool next to me.

"End of days, hoss. Not far off now," I said.

"Sad," he replied.

"Part of life, I suppose. But no, I don't like it either."

Bucket ordered identical to me and we took our drinks out

back into the dirt courtyard where a man with a cowboy hat stood DJing. One couple danced in the dirt and the others sat around in plastic chairs watching or talking or smoking or drinking or not doing anything at all.

"So how we gonna learn how to two-step?" Bucket asked me.

"Gonna ask one of these *abuelas* to teach us," I said.

"Bull."

"Just you watch, brother," I said, handing him my beer.

And that's exactly what I did. I walked right up to a pair of women, older women, not my mom's age but maybe like a younger sister of my mother. They were sitting down in their elegant dresses, hair piled high on top of their heads. They smiled at me, surprised, maybe thinking, the *cajones* on this *idiota*.

"*Baile, señora?*"

The one I asked looked at her friend, laughing. Then she took my extended hand and stood up. We started to dance in the dirt courtyard.

Needless to say, she was not impressed. But I think she could see that it was important to me, so without many words, she did her best to guide me. Not all of us have the desire or even the inclination to teach, I understood that. So I was grateful. To teach is to give something of yourself, and so many of us only ever want to indulge. But she was generous that night. The second song, she could've gone back to her lawn chair. But she kept dancing with me, and I liked to think I was getting better.

Over her shoulder, I could see Bucket, dancing with the other woman now. He had this big smile on his face, one of the biggest I'd ever seen him smile. He had one of those faces that couldn't lie about when he was having a good time. He looked to have about the same grace as me, but he had the same gratitude as me too, and his *tía* I think was happy that he was so tall and handsome. And I could see it in how she moved her hips, no matter her age. They moved with an unmistakable degree of mirth. Almost like she was showing off. No doubt, there was a level of joy in bestowing a lesson. Those were the final days of the Tejano bars in Austin. And we got the most of it. As much as we could.

Many years later, Bucket married a nice woman. A teacher. Isn't that something? He asked me to ordain the wedding. It was one of the most beautiful weddings I'd ever been to. I remember standing up at the altar with my friend, seeing what true happiness looked like, him, watching his future wife approach one step at a time. The relief that dawned upon this man's face. Like the night he learned to two-step, but times a thousand. That's how I knew. It was amazing.

Bucket had stayed in Austin. I'd left a long time ago, but here I was again, day after the wedding, at that Tejano bar, leaning on the counter, except it was no longer Tejano. Something else entirely now.

I was talking to the bartender and on my second round, a little resentful. Like I'd seen those Tejanos all those years back, regarding me with paltry malice. I knew I was being childish. And who I was talking to, this bartender, this kid, come down from Massachusetts. Clueless, hopeful, bought in on the American Dream. Another sucker.

"You know what this place was before this fancy cocktail bar?" I asked, the flashy garnishes of my Mai Tai hiding my lips.

"Some taco place?" the kid said.

"Some fucking taco place? Jesus Christ. It's a shame. It's a goddamn shame," I said, shaking my head.

"What's a shame?" someone asked.

I looked past the young bartender to a mountain of a man sitting on the other side of the bar. It was daytime and dark in the bar, but I could see he was Latino and had a goatee and a nice haircut and wore an Astros jersey.

I answered him. I said, "I liked this bar the way it was before. Do you remember?"

"I remember. I came up in this neighborhood."

"You don't miss it?" I asked him.

"Nah, homie. I don't miss it. I don't miss the gunshots. Worrying if my little brother would be safe to walk down the block. He can get a job now. I come back here now and see all the new things. It's beautiful. Not ugly how it was."

"I didn't think it was ugly," I said.

"Did you live here?"

"No," I said. "I didn't. I lived in the west side." I almost didn't want to admit that. But I wouldn't lie to the man.

"It was ugly," he told me. He didn't say it to prove anything to me. He said it like a man who had lived it, and of course, he had. "This is better. For everyone. Even you, *hermano*. Even if you don't know it yet."

I was quiet after that. I finished my drink, paid the bartender, walked around to the other side of the bar and put a fist up. The big guy put his fist to mine and smiled, absolute Buddha. I saw it. A confidence that came with wisdom. From having lived. I left the bar. The sun was still out. I put on my shades. I was confused about where I was for a second. A cab was lurching down the street. I hailed him and got back to my hotel. I was supposed to meet up with Bucket and a group of friends for dinner. I'd leave in the morning. I'd go back to the hotel and shower. Drink some water. Put on a nice shirt.

MY FRIEND OLLIE

Me and Rooster were making a name for ourselves at the restaurant. The chef only had himself to blame. He'd introduced us. We both had killer jean jackets and bad attitudes that everyone constantly forgave us for. I guess we were both just some charming motherfuckers. Almost every night we worked together, it was a given we'd be going out after to howl at the moon. We never invited anyone else and most were too timid to ask anyway. But somewhere along the line, Ollie started coming out with us too.

Now, I thought Ollie was drop dead gorgeous. But she seemed a little too neat by my standards. I didn't know why she'd want to come out with me and Rooster, cause it wasn't a secret that we were never up to any good. But that in itself looks attractive to some folk, you come to find out.

She'd ask, "What y'all doing tonight?"

I'd rear around to Rooster. He'd shrug. I looked back at Ollie.

"Drinking."

"Can I come?"

"OK," I said.

One night, we went to some bar on Red River. Downtown. Nastier than normal. This place was more of a club than a bar really. Wasn't one we frequented but that was the thing about me and Rooster. We could throw you a curve ball. You could describe us as versatile, I guess. I think, really, we just wanted to see what Ollie would do.

I ordered us a round of beers and a round of shots. Whiskey. Rail. We took the shots down first. Me and Rooster watched Ollie. She did good. I nodded to Rooster and leaned back against the counter, checking out the dance floor. It was completely empty, but the tunes were right.

"Ripe for the picking."

Rooster said what I was thinking. Ollie smiled big. She had on red lipstick. It went nice with her blond hair and the red gothic light.

We got out on the floor and started cutting a rug. Cutting it all up. We didn't care that we were the only ones. The DJ had INXS playing. I knew Rooster could dance but that night I found out Ollie could too. She wasn't too obvious about it either. Took her time. Sultry like. A Texas siren. We all happened to find a complimentary zone to coexist within. I was digging it.

The lights twirled hazy, dark red and blue, mixing together, changing the colors of our skin. We became creatures of the night, on the prowl, just as the big guy intended. "The big guy" Haha. I don't know why I said shit like that in Texas. Just seemed like a place he could hang out but still not give a fuck.

The three of us, though, we stayed in this rhythm, our faces mirroring each other, at times grinning, other times serious and dark, but always in the present, offering ourselves willingly and it was there and it was right.

Somewhere in there, these dudes showed up, some bro dudes, interrupting the groove, flocking around Ollie. She looked good and I guess they had their fill of liquid courage. I certainly thought it was brave of them. They were sort of shouting to her, trying to be heard over the volume of the song.

I don't know if they were New Austin, or Old Austin, but they were the Austin we tried to avoid, even though it was inevitable, because Austin was still Texas. Sharp haircuts and polos. Clean faces. White teeth. Me and Rooster instantly riled up. But it was Ollie.

She literally started barking at them. Barking loudly.

Arf! Arf! Arf!

Their faces resembled ours. Every man was shocked. But she was facing them. So it was they who were humiliated. They faded off, tails between their legs. She turned back to us, grinning like some crazy fucking thing. We hugged her tight, like we'd been waiting for her our entire lives.

It was Cyndi Lauper playing in the back ground. "All Through the Night." We stayed in a huddle and swayed like that, middle of the dance floor. We all went very far away. But all of us together.

And when we came back, we knew. All three of us. She was one of us now.

We went out all the time after that. Starting shit. Fighting. Lots of karaoke. Drugs, par for the course. Not even a blink. She was the most organized one about it. Go here. Talk to this guy. Rooster and I were happy to be directed. Funny how that works. Us, the top dogs, alpha males, take-shit-from-no-one motherfuckers. I couldn't wait for her to send me on an errand. I wanted to show up on her doorstep with the stuff in my mouth, wagging my tail big time.

"You like Ollie?" Rooster asked me one night as were driving to pick up an eight ball.

"Huh?" I said.

Rooster had a girlfriend. Always had. But he'd been a monster before then. I was single. Always had been in the minds and hearts of these present Texas folk. A lot of people couldn't wrap their heads around it.

"How come you don't got a sweetheart, Lev?" they'd asked me.

I never did have a good answer. That's honest. I guess, I just wasn't thinking with a mind towards it. It wasn't a priority. I felt sort of detached from everything, and being that way, every day I woke up I never felt like I owed anybody an apology. I was purely me.

Now, I did like attention. I just knew there was a lot of ways a person could get it. Good ways and bad ways.

"Do you like her?" Rooster repeated.

"The fuck kinda question is that? She's our sister, dude," I said.

"Uh huh," Rooster said, tapping his lip with a finger, his eyes on the road.

I was bothered by the question the rest of the night, but said nothing else, because I didn't know what else to say. I watched her do a line in a bathroom with red walls and when her head came up, her eyes were closed and she snapped her fingers twice and started nodding her head to a song I couldn't hear and put her index and pinkie finger up. Ollie was gorgeous and I loved her. It was true. But it wasn't like that. Hadn't ever been like that. But I could sort of admit. Maybe that seemed weird to some people. A guy liked a girl or he didn't, right? Rooster had a girlfriend, so he was exempt from the question but what about me? You get to a point. Does something romantic have to happen with the other gender just because you get along or can it really be platonic?

One night we went out, it was just the boys from the restaurant. Che was rolling with us. He wore glasses that had tape keeping them together in the middle and had more tattoos than Rooster and I put together. I knew Che was pretty rough around the edges, but so we were. Just sort of in different ways. Some men have different codes.

We stood in a parking lot next to Rooster's truck taking bumps before we rolled into the dance hall. We nodded to the door man as we walked in, the door man barely looking up from his phone as we passed him.

We got to the bar and got some whiskey, big pours. They knew us. We took them down but that cranked us up and not the easy way.

"Thinking about hitting the West Coast," Che said.

"For what?" Rooster asked.

"Switch it up. I been out here a minute now. Change of scenery be nice. New restaurant. New streets. New bitches."

"Yeah."

"You still with your old lady, Roose?"

"Yeah, man. 'Bout three years now."

"Whew," Che said. "What about you, Levy?"

"What's that?"

"You got anything going?"

"Nah. I'm cruising, brother."

"What about Ollie?"

"What about Ollie?" I repeated.

"You fucking her?"

I tilted my head at him. It felt like a fire was behind my eyeballs right away, but I kept my face cool. I acted like someone was asking me to pass the salt and pepper. "Nah. I ain't fucking her," I said.

"Why not? She's a fine piece of ass. I'd fuck her two ways from Sunday."

"Well, it ain't like that."

"What's it like then?"

"She's my friend."

Che started laughing. He looked out on the dance floor where the couples were two-stepping to a three-piece band. "What she up to tonight? Y'all usually run together anyway."

"Don't know," Rooster said.

"Huh," Che said. "I'ma walk around and see if there's anything in here to take a bite out of."

Che walked off. Rooster looked at me.

"You all right?"

"I'm fine," I said.

Rooster and I got a game of pool going. He won the first game, I won the second. We went into the bathroom to do some more bumps. Out back of the bar was a dirt yard with a taco truck. There was a half-built fence and along it, Che was whispering in some girl's ear. She must not have liked what he said cause she made a face and walked off. He leered after her. We came up to him.

"Man, let's jet this place. Ain't shit going on anyway," Che said, tossing an empty can of beer into the dirt.

"Band's all right," Rooster offered.

"I don't feel like dancing tonight. Shit, why don't you give me that ol' girl Ollie's number. See what she's up to tonight. If none of y'all are dicking her down, I ought to try my hand, ay?"

"Watch your fucking mouth," I said.

"What'd you say, boy?" Che said, squaring up fast.

"I ain't your boy. You talk some slick shit like that again . . ."

"And what?" he said, taking both his hands and shoving me.

I instantly dropped my can of beer and grabbed him by the wrists and whirled him around like I was swinging a tire to into my backyard. From the sudden and instinctive flashes of violence I'd participated in like this, I always surprised myself how much strength I possessed and how quick I was to yield it. Almost a childish astonishment, another me amazed at what my adult body was capable of. He flew into and through the half-built fence of the bar like he was in a Hollywood movie. Some girl shrieked behind me.

The door man appeared beside us. Very calmly, very politely, he said, "Y'all gonna have to leave."

"OK," I said.

Che was waiting in the parking lot. His clothes were all disheveled and his glasses were crooked, the tape barely holding on. Rooster got in front of him.

"I'm gonna dust you, faggot," Che told me.

"Told you to watch your mouth." I started walking off, not waiting for Rooster.

"The fuck is his problem?" I heard him say to Rooster.

I laid low for a couple nights. Didn't hang out with anyone, not even Rooster. Went to work, and after, I went to a different bar where I flew solo. I wasn't scared. I just had to be alone with my feelings. The weekend came. Ollie came up to me in the restaurant as the night was winding down.

"We going out tonight?"

"Seems appropriate," I said.

"Can I bring Leo?"

"Leo?" I said.

"Yeah."

I took a look at Leo, back in the kitchen. He was working on fry station that night. Truth be told, I liked Leo. He was a very nice boy from some part of Texas I'd never heard of nor would ever visit. I knew he had decent taste in music, a generally quiet guy that laughed at every joke I made. He was good looking but not obnoxiously so.

"OK," I said.

That night we went out, it was pretty easy to see Ollie and Leo had something working. He made her laugh a lot, which surprised me, though I found didn't make me mad. I liked seeing Ollie laugh. I caught Rooster watching me. I smiled and nodded at him.

"Y'all wolves need one?" Ollie asked, standing up.

"I'll take one," I said.

"Me too," Rooster said.

"Be right back," she walked off. It was just the three boys.

"I appreciate y'all letting me come out with you. I know y'all are some sort of a pack," Leo said.

Me and Rooster were quiet, smiling at him, not saying anything for a while. Finally, I said, "You're all right, Leo."

Ollie came back and handed out drinks. She sat down next to Leo. They started talking again. Me and Rooster got up and found a pool table, not too far away.

GATTACA

I knew my older brother Devonte had a different dad than I did, but I didn't know it by the difference of our skin color. I knew it because whenever my dad would piss him off by telling him to do something, or when they'd get into an argument, my older brother would later say angrily under his breath, "He's not my real dad."

I really hated when they would fight because I loved my older brother more than anything. Sometimes I was even the reason for why they would fight. Sometimes I would snitch. I hated to be a snitch, I knew you were never supposed to be one, but sometimes, as a little punk kid, it's the only weapon you have left to use. I'd hate to see him be punished, and maybe he wouldn't talk to me for a little while, but eventually I'd worm my way back into his good graces.

I think the first time I ever realized that we were different was when he was in high school. He might've already even been a senior. He was nine years older than me, he put gel in his hair to make it stand up, and I was able to understand that he was popular. I was just a pipsqueak in elementary school. One day, he brought a girl with blond hair home. Me and my two younger brothers were in the living room playing video games. Our parents weren't home. We put the game on pause to admire our brother. The girl was pretty.

"Who are these little cutie pies?" the girl giggled at us. We were quiet, shy, bushy-haired brown little boys who had no idea in the world how to talk to girls or even just act normal. To be honest, I don't think I could barely look a girl in the eyes yet.

"Those are my little brothers," Devonte told her.

She giggled again, pushing his arm playfully. Even her eyes seemed to smile at him. "No really," she said.

"I'm for real. Those are my little brothers," he repeated.

Then she tilted her head, the reality of it dawning on her. Whatever her reality might have been.

She just said, "Oh." Then they went upstairs.

Me and my younger brothers started playing video games again. Eventually, my youngest brother asked, "How come that girl didn't believe Dev?"

"What do you mean?" my other brother said.

"How come she didn't believe him when he said we're his brothers?"

"Because Devonte is white. And we aren't," I said. I tossed my controller to my youngest brother and got off the couch. I left my little brothers to go walk around the neighborhood and be by myself. I was upset. I didn't know why, all I knew was I'd learned by then when I felt this way it was better to just go off on my own.

There'd be these times when my dad would be mad and we'd never have any idea why. He didn't do it all the time, but sometimes he might take it out on us, brief hot moments that left us speechless. I hated him in those moments. So even by my young age, I knew I never wanted to be that way. Sometimes I'd walk so damn far off by myself, I'd find myself completely lost. But somehow, I always found my way back home.

■

I was in high school and the day had finished. Hour ride back home in the yellow bus, I kept my head against the window, headphones on, blasting M.O.P. I found I was angry a lot. I had this indescribable energy, and the only way I knew how to release it was through some physical outlet. Maybe there was another way, but there wasn't anyone for me to communicate this with, so I was stuck with it. I didn't know why I was this way. I didn't understand it. But then, nobody asked me to. So I just went through the motions. Pass the bullshit placement tests, save my antics for when I couldn't get suspended. I didn't learn how to talk to girls until I started drinking. And even then, we weren't really talking.

The bus dropped me off only a block from my house. Walking up, I saw Devonte's Taurus in front. My older brother didn't live with us anymore, didn't even live in the same state. I hopped up the steps excitedly.

Everyone was in the kitchen, standing and sitting around Dev as he ate a sandwich and had a glass of water. Everyone was quiet, listening to him talk.

"It hasn't been easy. Getting a foot in the door. Weird interactions I wasn't ready for. But I'm getting there. Just gotta stay on track," Devonte was saying.

"Weird why?" my youngest brother asked.

"Interviewing for work, starting a job, and there's this . . . this awkwardness. Like some wall. It's hard to explain. Maybe just cause I'm the new guy."

He finally saw me and nodded his head and smiled. I smiled back even though I didn't mean to. I didn't *not* want to, it just happened without me thinking about it, and I felt like maybe it made my face look dumb. I was trying to grow a mustache. It wasn't going well.

"Give your older brother a hug," my mom commanded me.

He stood up and we hugged. He took a look at me.

"Baggy jeans, boy," Devonte said to me. I just shrugged and smiled stupidly again. I left them in the kitchen and went upstairs up to my room where I closed the door. I stayed up there, listening to music, until mom called everyone for dinner. We usually sat in the TV room, watching some show, no one talking, probably preferable. But Dev was home, so we sat at the dinner table. A more traditional and performative family this evening. Everyone was asking him stuff about life in the south, as they ought to have, but I just ate my food. When I finished, I asked to be excused. I went back up to my room.

Even back then, I was already staying up late. My parents hated that I did, but I finally had my own room so there wasn't anyone to stop me. The stairs creaked like hell when anyone stepped on them, but I knew most of the ones that gave you trouble and did my best to avoid them. I wanted a glass of Kool-Aid. I could see the blue light from the TV room. I went to the kitchen, poured myself a glass, and found my older brother sitting on the couch by himself.

He looked at me, not smiling, almost like he'd been expecting me. I stood in the doorway.

"You ever seen this movie before?" he asked me.

"What is it?"

"*Gattaca.*"

I sat down with him. I recognized the actor. Ethan Hawke. He was standing on a beach with another man.

"What's happening?" I asked my brother.

"They're brothers, and they want to see how far they can swim into the water. They want to see which one of them gives up first. One of the brothers, he's engineered. He's supposed to be better."

"A better swimmer?"

"Just better. In everything. He was engineered to be better."

"Is he?"

"No," Devonte said. "Some things go beyond science."

I didn't understand everything about the movie but I knew I liked it. When it was finished, Devonte and I hugged again, longer than before. Then he lay down on the couch and turned off the TV. The couch was his bed that night.

I woke up late the next day. No one bothered me. It was the weekend. When I came downstairs, my mom was sitting at the table in the kitchen, reading the paper. I could see into the TV room. No one was in there. The blankets were gone.

"Where's Dev?" I asked.

"He already left," she told me, not looking up from the paper.

■

We were walking down this street and it was late, this girl and me. I was in college. We were drunk and we were laughing softly, laughing into each other's neck and hair and collar bone, stumbling towards my place. It was one of those rare nights where things go better than you could have expected. Two people ready to fall into each other. Maybe she'd known all along. But it definitely seemed like we were both pretty excited, excited like kids really. Giddy. She had both her arms around my waist and my arm was over her shoulder, and she had her head in my chest. Her dark hair covered her eyes but I could see her grinning.

"What is it?" I asked her.

"Nothing," she said, giggling.

"Tell me."

"I've never hooked up with a black guy before," she said. "I just never thought I was the type."

She said it with such blind honesty, an almost innocence to it, like a child saying a curse word for the first time. And the whole room just laughing. Mom and dad, uncle and aunt. The pseudo shade of innocence was the only thing that allowed me to continue to walk. To not abruptly halt in my tracks, to erupt with emotion. It was a wild moment where I didn't know what to do, didn't know what to say. It wasn't the first time I'd ever experienced a moment like this, the shock, but also, it was even familiar in a way. It was familiar because by then I enjoyed doing the same thing to white people. Freezing them with such a loaded statement they would be completely unsure of how to proceed, until they would see my gradual smile reveal itself, allowing them to sink back into comfort, maybe wag their finger at me. *You got me*, maybe they'd say. But the difference was, I did it on purpose. This girl, this sweet girl. This sweet stupid fucking girl. She was genuinely looking forward to this novel experience. She was very pretty.

"Come on, I'm right up here," I said, pulling the keys out of my jeans.

Fuck it, I thought. I'm getting laid tonight.

■

My mother never told us why she gave us the names she did. Or maybe we never asked. We had to have asked. At some point. I don't remember asking. But I know she was always evasive with her answers anyway. So I can't remember. We all had such different names. My mother was secretly very romantic, despite her tough exterior. She had a ton of stories but a lot of times the only ones she'd share were ones to scare us with, to keep us in line, I'm sure passed down to her from her own jerk father. She told us stories to make sure we didn't get anyone pregnant, stories to stay away from liquor, stories not to fight with cops. All things she'd done rampantly in her youth. Now that I was older, I guess I could respect reserving the more adventurous stories. She wanted us to be better. God bless her.

Devonte was living in Raleigh. College was over and I was in between jobs, or that's what I told my parents. I borrowed their car and drove down from Virginia to my older brother's and never told my dad my license had been suspended. The drive was a straight shot, smooth. I'd made it a million times with the Baker brothers, sitting shotgun tossing silver Nattys into the black wind like a scumbag.

I pulled into Devonte's apartment parking lot. I could see him right away, leaning against the railing of his balcony, a cigarette hanging off his lip. He was shirtless and he had his hair buzzed, just like me. Except, of course, when he grew his hair out, it wouldn't be a curly afro. It would be straight and brown.

I parked and got out the car with my bag. He gave me a curt salute, flicked the cigarette, and went inside his apartment. He met me at the bottom of the stairs. He smiled, just a sliver of his teeth showing. Forever the prince of wolves.

We hugged and didn't say a word to each other until we got upstairs. He opened the door to a room.

"This is you," he said. I looked inside. I tossed my bag on the bed and nodded to him.

"Wanna check out the pool?" he asked.

"OK."

"You got trunks?"

"Nah," I told him.

"I got some you can borrow."

It was a good-sized pool, and clean. No one was out there except a mom and her kid. The kid had those little orange floaties tied to his arms. I dived in. When I came up, Devonte was sitting on a chair, starting another cigarette.

"Bunch of tattoos, boy," he said to me. "Mom know?"

"She knows about some of 'em."

"What she say?"

"She don't like 'em."

Devonte laughed quietly, ashing his cigarette. "Well anyway, how you feeling?"

"This feels nice. But I'm tired," I said.

"When you come out, take a quick nap maybe. My girl's coming over tonight. Want you to meet her. I'm cooking dinner. Stuff Mom makes."

"OK," I said. I swam a couple laps, lazily, mostly floating. It felt peaceful. The sun had that good southern heat to it, the distant sizzle. Submerged, the humidity couldn't touch me. The light was cutting up off the water so that I had to squint. The little boy on the other side of the pool was loving life. His mother looked on him with a lot of care. It was pleasant to witness.

We went upstairs and I rinsed off the chlorine in the shower, then I took that nap. I fell asleep almost immediately. When it was time, Devonte woke me up. He wasn't an asshole about it. He opened the door and he called my name softly until I opened my eyes.

"Come on," he said. "Dinner's ready."

I came out the bedroom rubbing my eyes. There was a young lady leaning against the wall next to the kitchen, her arms crossed. She was smiling at me. It was a nice smile. Like if I saw it in a grocery store from a stranger, I would smile back, would feel good about smiling back. I'd hope she'd found everything she came in that grocery store looking for. But I realized this was the woman my brother had invited over for dinner. To meet his younger brother. So I didn't smile. I nodded to her.

"Hi," I said, monotone.

She put out a hand. "So nice to meet you. Collin's told me so much about you."

Her hand hung there, in the air. I looked at Devonte, not understanding. He was looking at me, not saying anything, but his expression was serious and he was looking me right in the eyes. I wanted to repeat the name she'd said. But I saw something in his eyes. I finally shook her hand.

"Yeah," I said. "I'm sure Collin has."

Devonte made the plates for all three of us. We sat around a low glass table, in front of the TV. There was small conversation but no one was really saying very much. The food was very good. He'd made it just like mom. I was impressed but remained silent. I felt like I was right back home. Mom and Dad. Amazing, how they held it together all those years. Devonte's girlfriend seemed nice enough. She wasn't apathetic. She wasn't defensive. She asked decent questions, but she also wasn't a dummy. She could tell what I was doing.

We finished eating dinner and then sat around watching some stand up. Devonte's girlfriend had a nice laugh and it seemed genuine. I stood up.

"I'm gonna float around the pool a little more," I said. "Nice to meet you," I told his girlfriend.

We shook hands again, politely, formally.

I went into my room and got my borrowed trunks and a towel and went back down to the pool. There were lights on but I would've been fine in the dark anyway. I sank into the water, all the way in, until I was gone. I began to finally feel calmer. I'd come up from the water, but with my face only, just to breathe. Then I'd submerge again. I stayed down there, holding my breath, as long as I could, until my chest seemed ready to burst.

I was down there, watching the bubbles rise to the surface, when overhead, I could see the wavering figure of who I assumed was my older brother. I came up, pulling myself to the edge of the pool. Devonte was standing there.

"You mad at me?" he asked me.

"For what?"

"You know what," he said, hands on his hips. "Didn't know how to tell you. Kind of forgot, to be honest."

"Forgot you were a completely different person than my brother? That you just made up someone to be?" I asked him.

He sighed, looking away. "I'm not a different person, boy. It's just a name. It's complicated."

"Yeah, whatever," I said, pulling myself out of the pool. I grabbed my towel and started to walk away. He grabbed my brown arm. I glared at him, everything in my eyes saying I was this close to throwing a right hook. Devonte stood his ground.

"You're gonna listen to me," he said firmly.

We sat down on some chairs next to the glowing pool. My jaw was clenched the whole time. I stared at my feet. My head was too heavy to look any higher.

"It's fucked up," he started. "I finished school. Top of my class. Should've got me a job right away. Took me forever. I couldn't figure it out." He lit two cigarettes. He handed one of them to me. I accepted and took a drag immediately.

"I didn't notice it until one of the interviews. Felt so dumb after. Guy said to me, "Oh, wow. By your name, you weren't what we were expecting." That's when I got it. You see what I'm saying?"

"They thought you were black," I said.

"Right," Devonte said. "So I conducted an experiment. I made up a name. A white sounding name."

My head was lifting higher. I could hear cars far off. My skin was prickling in the night air. I tapped my cigarette.

"Put Collin on my applications. Started to get called back a lot more. More jobs. What's funny, I guess, was I just started using the name whenever. If I was out, with friends, meeting people. Any time at all. No one knew any better. No one knows me here. I made this whole life. All I had to do was say it. Hey, I'm Collin. Everything seemed . . . easier."

I took the last drag off my cigarette. I made it last. I flicked it into the pool. I could tell he didn't like that by how his body jerked up, but he didn't say anything.

"Well, I'm glad to hear life got easier for you, brother," I said, standing up.

"Now, wait a second," he said. "I know."

"No," I said. "You don't. That's the point. I don't have it so easy. It's not just a name change for me. I can't just take this off," I said, pulling at the skin on my brown arm.

"This isn't me against you," he told me.

"You're supposed to be my brother," I said back. I could feel tears running down my cheek. I knew it had been a long time since I'd felt them. They were hotter than I remembered. They lasted longer, running down my no longer child face.

"Hey. What the hell. I always will be." He was holding on to my arm again.

We went back upstairs. His girl was no longer there. He pulled out a handle of tequila from the cabinet above his refrigerator, along with two shot glasses. We then began to get aggressive. Which was familiar. Even welcoming. We punched each other. Grinned. Reminisced about memories many others would find traumatic, and maybe they were, but we just laughed about them now. He hugged me and I hugged him back and I didn't want to let go but finally I did.

I woke up before he did. As in, the door to his bedroom was still closed when I went to use the bathroom.

I used the toilet, brushed my teeth, rubbed cold water on my face. Then I packed my stuff up, made my bed like mom taught me to, and left my older brother Devonte's place. The sun was bright. I put on my sunglasses. When I got into the car, I looked up at my brother's balcony. He was up there, no shirt, lighting a cigarette. He gave me the same curt salute from when I'd arrived. I started the car and lowered the window. I held my hand up. Then I pulled out of the lot and drove away.

A FEELING HARD TO EXPLAIN

Alaine and I were both off that night from the restaurant and said we'd meet up for drinks, just 'cause, except this time the location was her choice. I said OK 'cause last time I'd taken her to a nasty old dive, and it'd been a shit show. We'd still had fun, but it was clear it was not her scene, not through her discomfort or complaint, because she'd exhibited neither, but simply because the next day she'd said, "What a shit show."

I wouldn't have disagreed. I gave her props for sticking it out because not all my friends did stuff like that. I knew Alaine was a classy kind of chick. She had an air of knowing what it was about. The whole game. But she wasn't a snob. She just knew things. She was from Baltimore. She could be rough. I knew because sometimes I'd talk shit, you know, when I drank too much, which was often those days. Maybe sort of these days too. But with her, if it went too far, she put me in my place and I could feel the danger in her tone. I could feel it like a knife on my Adam's apple. And I knew to step back, relax my tenor of my voice, maybe say something nice, like you're right or I'm sorry or I'm an idiot. And when the knife left my skin, I could look her in the eyes again and see this white girl who was very pretty and sometimes goofy with how her nose twitched when she was thinking about something, but undercover very dangerous and always, always sincere.

I walked into the bar and it was dark, which I liked, but it was lit up too. Just lit up a different kind of way. The lights felt like they were star beams from outer space, and for the women who were in there, the light made their dresses kind of sparkle and radiate in a way I wasn't accustomed to. All the men looked good too, nice fitting pants and chiseled haircuts and enthusiastic expressions. The bar glowed and it seemed like a place that if you approached you needed to be prepared to order and order properly. I saw Alaine sitting at the bar, her sharp short haircut. She looked good. She always did. I sat down next to her.

"Not so bad huh?" she said.

"It's awful," I replied.

She laughed. She had a great laugh. That's such an underrated thing in a person, I thought. A good laugh can make you turn your head. Make you laugh yourself. Make you fall in love.

But that wasn't what this was about. And I wasn't sure why, to be honest. I could think to myself, well, this is the second time we're meeting up for drinks, just us. Shouldn't I try? But it was more of a feeling. A feeling hard to explain. I liked Alaine. I liked being around her. Did I find her attractive? Sure. But I didn't feel it hot. And that was a different thing to think about all together. Did I have to feel that to want it? Was that what wanting it was about?

I could've also wondered what she was here for. She could've been anywhere. I turned from her and looked into the eyes of my awaiting bartender.

"What would you like?"

"A sidecar, please."

The bartender nodded and turned away to her task.

"So this is your spot, huh?" I asked her.

"One of them," she answered.

I looked at her sideways and she let that laugh spill out again. I laughed a little too, shaking my head. The drink came to me and I thanked the bartender and sipped from the sugar encrusted coupe and the drink was exactly what I had in mind.

"Good?" Alaine asked, watching me.

I just shrugged.

It wasn't that I felt underdressed but rather that everyone in the room could tell my clothes weren't as expensive. Therefore, I felt more like a visitor. A tourist. Nothing wrong with being a tourist, but there were different ways to receive a tourist in different parts of the world. And this part of the world, a tourist had to have something to offer. And by my clothes alone, even in my cool jean jacket, the up and down look I got from anyone that I passed translated to my value being little to nothing. But then again, this was just all in my head. But also, fuck these punks.

I focused back on Alaine. "What'd you do on your day off today?"

"Laundry. Some emails. Trying to lock this thing down in NYC."

"Oh yeah?"

"Can't wait tables forever."

"I know that's right."

"What about you?"

"I had a long night last night so . . ."

"Can you remember the last time you had a short one?"

"Only thing I'm short on is patience."

"Shut the fuck up," Alaine said. More laughing.

I really think the laughing was our connector. I was asked once if I had friends I didn't laugh with, and the answer was yes. I'm not saying we never ever *didn't* laugh, but the entire reason we kept company was founded on something else entirely. The relationship provided some other kind of sustenance maybe.

Laughter wasn't the singular point. But with Alaine, laughter was the point. I don't think she would've liked me very much if we didn't laugh so much. I don't know that we had a lot of other things in common, come to think about it.

"Why do you like places like this?" I asked her, crossing my arms and slouching.

"What's wrong with a place like this? The atmosphere is cool. They make great cocktails. I don't have to look to see if there's slime in my seat. What do you got against a place like this?"

"Just ain't for me," I answered defiantly.

"What's for you? Those grimy dives you're always in? Hanging out with a bunch of grandpas that are always saying some nasty shit about any woman that walks by? Bathrooms you can smell before you even walk into the bar? Plastic cups?"

I straightened in my seat, jutting my bottom lip out. Alaine started laughing again. I relaxed, just a little. I whirled a single finger around.

"You think you would really want to have a conversation with any of these twerps in here?"

"You think I wanna talk to a guy with a beer belly so big he can't see his own dick, with grease on his shirt?"

"Who do you wanna talk to?" I asked her.

"Sometimes I don't want to talk at all, Levy. Sometimes I just want to have a nice drink and listen to music and stare at my phone. And then, you know what?"

"What?"

"Then just go to sleep. 'Cause I'm only twenty-five. And I'm already fucking tired, all the time."

We stared at each other a while, not saying anything. The bartender came by again.

"Drinks OK?" she asked us.

Alaine and I both smiled, then turned to the bartender.

"Excellent, miss," I said. I held my glass up to Alaine and she lifted hers.

FOUR BLACK GUYS
GET INTO A CAR

The four of us hopped into a silver Acura. Darnell's. It was all banged up, paint job scorched. It didn't look great. Not a one of us cared. Somebody had a car, that's all that mattered. I took shotgun. With all the CD cases littering the floor, my feet never touched the mat. The clutter was inconceivable to me. I grew up in a military family, a big family too. Messes were not tolerated. Not by the parents, the kids, even the dogs. If the dog made a mess, my dad would put his nose in it. It wasn't much different with the kids. That was our conditioning. So now my mind couldn't work right if my own space was too crazy. But this wasn't my space. Darnell didn't seem to care. I dug my shoes into the sandpit of CDs. I had to scoot my seat up because Vash had long legs. Maybe it was a little cruel of me to make him sit in the back seat but maybe I was a little cruel back then, cruel in that I wanted my presence to be recognized, no matter who it hurt. Young and cruel and anxious to prove it.

We were on our way to a party but for the first time ever, the four of us had decided to meet up beforehand, listen to some music, good music, and hang out before the madness ensued. It was nice. Very natural. I wished I'd recognized that more at the time, the notion of something feeling right, but when you are young you just want to be cool and being cool a lot of times involves not paying attention to feelings, and not paying attention to feelings ensures you taking for granted the quality of your life and the relationships that could've blossomed into something much more radiant. How would you be remembered all the years later? So many times, just another body in an old photograph. Anyway, we'd had a nice time at that pre-party, listening to music, laughing, playing some video games, not under anyone's inspection. Safe.

Once Darnell started the car, I looked back and around, looking at Darnell, Vash, and Rizzo.

"Holy shit," I laughed, "besides when I'm with fam, this is the first time I've been in the car with all black motherfuckers."

One of those long but at the same time fast seconds passed, everyone silent in the car, allowing the reality of my ridiculous statement to register. Then everyone started laughing hard. I didn't know if they were laughing because it was true for them too or because I sounded like such a damn fool, but I know the way the laughter sounded, it didn't make me feel ashamed. It didn't make me feel like an alien.

We were at the tail end of college by then. I'd known Vash the longest. Vash didn't know his dad. His mom had a job with the government. It had taken me a while to get to like Vash, but at some point, I'd realized we'd just been raised wholly different. It's a trip when you think everyone was raised the same way you were and then you find out like some giant revelation in the world that they weren't. It makes you feel like your face is on some giant poster to show everybody what an idiot looks like. The ironic thing is so many people don't actually get there, to that understanding. They think their world is the same for everyone. That's why they get so confused. That's why they can be so ruthless. So many people can't conceive of problems they themselves have never experienced. That's why it can be so easy for some to walk by a man sitting on a street corner on a freezing afternoon.

I grew to feel a great affection towards Vash because of how big he laughed and because I could grab him and hold on to him and shake him, and all he'd do is laugh, laugh, laugh, which was the only thing I wanted. It was like we'd grown up together, but we hadn't. That was just the feeling. I couldn't do that with most other friends. They'd feel uncomfortable, maybe even alarmed. They weren't used to that kind of physicality. That level of affection or joy communicated through the body. But when I'd do that to Vash, he'd just laugh. Real loud. So everyone would look at us and see us laughing and smiling. He'd never push me off him or act awkward. Sometimes people look at us like they were confused. Imagine being confused over something like that. Imagine something like joy being foreign to you.

Darnell had actually been set up to be my rival when we were first introduced. I don't think either of us had been excited about that but we followed our allegiances, played by the rules, *their* rules, until we recognized the rules were all made up, and that it was perfectly fine to just be cool with each other. You see, we were the token black guys in our respective crews. So we were just expected to be adversaries. What a sudden and massive relief it was to just say fuck that.

And lo and behold, all the things we had in common. I was happy to find I could learn a lot from Darnell. A real smart guy, but low key. He knew the city well and the people knew him too. It was interesting that he came from a well-to-do family because in spite of that, he still chose to hang out with people like us, out in the street, in the dark and in the gutter. Driving us around in this beat-up Acura when we all knew he could have something a lot nicer.

And finally, there was Rizzo. Darnell brought Rizzo in. I'd seen him around on campus. He had a very identifiable and meticulously shaped afro. Huge really, like a perpetual ebony cloud crowning his head, following him wherever he went. He was probably the most naturally cool out of us. He just had this fluid quality, he just seemed to glide everywhere. I think Rizzo was probably the one with the least to prove from our ranks. He was an artist, one of the first real ones I'd ever known, and he was an encyclopedia of music and history and he didn't care about any bullshit like popularity or brands or who was friends with who or who was fucking who. Rizzo was just Rizzo. Rizzo always had a girlfriend and he only dated white girls. Just like the rest of us.

And why was that?

Well, we never talked about that. But I'm sure we all wondered. I don't think it was an exclusive taste for any of us. I found all sorts of women attractive and I didn't have any problem saying so or acting on it when the opportunity arose. But whenever I'd introduce an actual girlfriend . . . well that was all the proof anybody needed, wasn't it? I don't know if it made any of the other boys feel ashamed. I'd never asked. And they never said anything either. But I'm sure the thought crossed their minds.

For instance, I thought it was funny Vash had a provocative pin up of a voluptuous black girl with an afro on his forearm. Where was she? I never asked. Probably because I didn't want to be asked right back. None of us wanted to be asked. None of us knew the answer.

I might have had some ideas, as I flipped through a magazine in a waiting room where they'd given the title of sexiest woman to Scarlett Johansson. As I looked up on a friend's wall to see a poster of *Final Fantasy VII*, one of my favorite video games, with one of its main characters Tifa standing front and center with her hands on her hips and her lily-white complexion and giant bosom. As I grew up watching Madonna and Paula Abdul dance and laugh and frolic in their music videos. As I grew up watching movies like *Save the Last Dance* and *Finding Forrester* and *Jungle Fever* and as I dug out *Playboy* and *Hustler* magazines from my neighbor's garage.

So maybe the reason we laughed over my idiotic proclamation was actually quite simple. We'd all four, not just Darnell and I, started out as the token black guy in our respective backgrounds. It was a crazy thing to secretly realize, to think much less say out loud, but whether someone wanted to say it or think it or do neither didn't make it any less true. Here were the four of us, in some alternate dimension, oblivious to our destinies. Or were we? You could trace where we'd been raised and how. Maybe that wouldn't reveal the journey to this coincidence. Maybe it wasn't coincidence at all. We were in college now. We could have chosen to seek our own and our own only right from the gate. Complete immersion. But it isn't quite that easy, is it? You spend your life growing up trying to incorporate all these things in your life, to have the most, to know the most. I'd grown accustomed to having the freedom to like whatever I wanted, pursue any interest I'd have, and without much judgment. You know, like white people are able to. What a simple thing, and yet there were certainly times I'd had to remember my freedom was in fact limited. That my choices could in fact be judged harshly or even denied. Or maybe not even harshly. Maybe not in any mean-spirited kind of way at all. But you know it. You see it in their eyes.

I remember during middle school, I had this friend in the neighborhood, the only other black kid. He lived just down the block from me. We'd take the bus and sit next to each other every day. High school started, and our paths diverged. He came over one day during high school and I hadn't been expecting him, he'd just shown up to the house. I was happy to see him. Now that we didn't have the bus, we didn't see each other often at all. We went up to my room. He turned on my stereo to play the radio and before I could do anything about it, some rock music started blaring. I tried to change the channel immediately. I didn't know why. But of course, I knew why. My face maybe resembled a computer screen when the page you're loading gets frozen. He grinned at me. He didn't say a damn thing. He knew. And I knew. I don't know where that boy ended up.

I ended up in Richmond, Virginia.

I didn't know all the details of how Rizzo or Vash or Darnell grew up, but I knew we were all very happy to be friends that night and to be hanging out and in a different way than how we hung out with our general friend groups. We couldn't talk about it. Not yet. It was just a feeling. A really good feeling. It was right there with us in that Acura.

We started to move and Darnell put on his stereo. Björk started to play.

"Not exactly party music," Darnell offered.

"What you want then?"

"Maybe some Neptunes."

"Or maybe we could just go beast-mode with some Earth Crisis," I said, holding up the CD case from the pile I was sitting on.

"Fuck yes," Rizzo said from the back.

I handed the CD to Darnell, who was grinning like hell. He slipped the disc in and the car transformed into the Thunderdome. All four of us began to thrash the vehicle. Raw blistering youth.

We swept through the city, weaving our way downtown. We got to a red light and a song had just finished climatically. Darnell turned down the volume.

"Levy, didn't you used to live in Iceland?"

"Yeah. Why you bring that up?" I asked.

"Björk. Reminded me of it."

"Oh right."

"What was that like?" Rizzo asked from the back.

"You know, I know Iceland's supposed to be popular now with all its tourism and shit. They got some cool shit up there, I guess. Blue Lagoons and whatnot. Some very decent bird watching available. Puffins and shit."

"Oh, you like birds?" Darnell said.

"Oh yeah, man. Big into birds. Big time. Remind me to tell you about my uncle and his black market bird business sometime. But anyhow, that place was actually wack as fuck."

"Why you say that?"

"Icelandics, at least when I was there in the late '80s, well, I'll put it like this: They were basically Europe's version of rednecks."

"Whoa, for real?"

"For real. I mean, think about it. I don't know how much y'all know about Iceland, but the people who settled there, they were specifically setting themselves up not to be fucked with by anybody, you know? That's why they named Iceland, Iceland and Greenland, Greenland."

"Oh shit, I heard about that," Darnell said.

"Yeah. Misdirection, my dude. They didn't want anything to do with anybody else. And for a long time, they didn't have to. So you can imagine the inbreeding going on."

"Damn," Vash said.

"Maybe that's unfair of me to say . . . but I don't think it's *not* true. Anyhow, America says, you know what, we need a pit stop on our way flying to Europe, so we'll plop a base down on this Iceland. Call it Keflavik."

"And the capital's Reykjavik," Rizzo said.

"Yup. I don't know if that pissed them off or not. I just know my older brother went off base in his senior year of high school with his buddies. Legal drinking age is only 18 there, you know."

"OK. And?"

"The Icelandics didn't appreciate the diversity of my brother and his friends."

"What happened?"

"He came back home with his face looking like that fucked up dude from *The Goonies*."

"Damn!" they all echoed in the car in unison.

"My brother's my fucking idol. I've never forgiven those bastards," I said, looking out the window. It was quiet in the car a while. Finally, I said, "But you know, I love Björk. And that movie she was in. *Dancer in the Dark*. Amazing. I'll never watch it again besides the one time, but real good."

"That movie was fucked up," Rizzo said.

"It really was," Darnell agreed.

Darnell was coming up on a light that had just turned yellow. He was slowing down, but at the last second, I saw a police car. I stiffened in my seat instinctively, and whispered loudly but calmly, "Cops."

Darnell stopped the car at the red light. Everyone got very quiet. Darnell even lowered the volume again. The four of us watched the police car slowly cross the intersection. It disappeared into the night like a shark in a black sea.

"It's all good, man. We don't have anything in the car and I haven't had anything to drink tonight. We're good," Darnell chuckled.

"Yeah. I know," I said. "But you know."

Everyone chuckled but not because what I said was funny. Maybe that was some additional conditioning there. Either way, Darnell turned the music back up. Soon we arrived at our destination. We parked and got out the car and shed the skin of fear we'd so instantly, instinctively grown. There was a line going down the block to the club and some of our friends saw us. They pointed and started hollering. We were all kings again.

IDOLS PART SIX

My mom was driving me to the airport this time. Usually it was my dad. So, in my mind, I'm thinking: This is growth. Me and her are coming along. Goddamn, it hadn't been easy. I had a suitcase and a big taped up cardboard box with my bike in it. That's it. That was my whole life at the time. All I needed.

"Where'd you get that jacket?" she asked, barely looking over at me.

"What? This?" I said.

I'd just gotten the jean jacket a couple weeks before in a thrift store. I'd never had one before. I'd been watching a lot of movies from the '80s. It seemed like the right time. I was ready for the next step.

"I just got it," I said.

My mom kind of snickered.

"What?" I said.

She didn't take her eyes off the highway. "When I was a kid, the Beatles came to Amsterdam. They were playing by the canals. Remember when I took you to the canals? Anyway, it drove everybody crazy, them being there. The parents hated it. All the kids were jumping into the water."

I looked at her, grinning, because I knew how rare it was for her to share any childhood gems. I was eating it up.

"I was one of those kids. Had a jean jacket just like that. Never saw it again," she told me.

We got to the airport.

"You coming in with me?" I asked, the door hanging up.

"No," she told me. "And do yourself a favor."

"What?" I asked, feeling bummed.

"Save your money," she said.

"For what?" I asked her.

"You never know. Come on, get out, there's people behind us."

NAH, I'M GOOD

Kamaru and Claire were getting married. They'd moved back to the city where they'd all grown up, and where her parents still lived. Kamaru had achieved his goal and become a dentist. He was making good money and he'd only just started. Claire had a job, but they all knew the next step was for her to get pregnant and be a mom. And that was a nice thing. She'd be a great mother.

Rome flew into Virginia Beach the day before the wedding from Chicago. He'd had to connect in D.C. Kamaru picked him up from the airport. When he got there, he came out of the car and walked around and gave Rome a big hug.

"We're so glad you could make it," he told him.

That stuck out to Rome. That natural way of saying "we." It made him smile.

"Wouldn't miss it for the world, brother," Rome said.

"Where you staying?" Kamura asked when they got into the car.

"Holiday Inn. I'll give you directions."

As they drove, Kamaru leaned back in his seat with one hand on the wheel, the other hand massaging his chin. Rome observed him quietly a while, then started laughing. Kamaru looked over, grinning.

"What?"

"Nothing. Tell me, you nervous?"

"Nah, man. I mean, maybe. It's been leading up to this forever, right? Feels like forever."

"Yeah."

"So really, I'm just doing what I always said I would. And that feels good. Feels . . . right. But what's up with you? How's Chicago been?"

"Great, man. Great. Work is good. Just those winters."

"Brutal, huh?"

"The most brutal thing."

They pulled up to the hotel. Rome got out and pulled out his luggage and garment bag from the back. He leaned down into the passenger window.

"So you can make it to dinner?" Kamaru asked.

"Yeah. I'll Uber over. Eight o'clock?"

"You got it, buddy. Claire wants to do karaoke after. You still got it?"

"Oh, baby. I ain't never lost it."

Kamaru grinned and pulled the car away. Rome checked into the hotel.

The rehearsal dinner was at some seafood place Rome had never been to before though he'd always seen the sign. They'd gotten a private room in the back. Two big tables. The lighting was nice. White linen on the tables, flowers in crystal vases set symmetrically. Everyone who was there was standing up with a cocktail in their hand. The staff, all dressed in black, stood discreetly along the sides of the room with their hands placed professionally behind their back. One of them greeted Rome as soon as he entered and handed him a small drink menu. He picked the old fashioned and she left to go retrieve it. Claire appeared in front of him, a lovely dress on, and all smiles. They hugged warmly. He always forgot how tall she was, even more so in heels. She introduced him to her parents, who were somehow quite short but more to what he would have in mind for a Filipino family. They said little, maybe somewhat overwhelmed with all the hands they were having to shake, but unmistakably happy for their daughter and basking in the joy that surrounded them. They glowed with it.

Kamaru's parents were the only ones sitting. They'd just driven in from Philadelphia. It was where Kamaru's dad was from and they'd returned there after he'd retired. You could tell they were spent but they were just as happy for their son. Rome sat with them once he'd gotten his drink, taking the opportunity to catch up. They'd always been good to Rome and told him they were happy to see him there.

Rome looked up and saw Rueben walk in. He tried to act like he didn't. He kept talking to Kamaru's parents.

"It gets cold up there, don't it?" Kamaru's father said to him.

"It's no competition, but yeah, a lot colder than Philly. It's no joke."

"We should've stayed down here. It's too cold in Philly," Kamuru's mom complained.

His dad grumbled, then said, "Hope that job is worth it, son."

"Yeah, that and the summer. It's worth it. For now," he answered.

Claire went to the front of the room and put her hands up.

"Okay, everybody, thank you so, so much for getting here. I think we're all here now, so we're gonna start! There are cards with your names on it placed just above the plates, so find where you are, settle in, and enjoy yourselves."

Thoughtful of her, Rome thought to himself. Claire had always been pretty aware that way. Considerate that way. He shook Kamaru's parents hands and stood up. He deliberately kept his eyes down, scanning for his name, casually avoiding Rueben's gaze. He found his seat at the end of a table, next to another couple he knew and liked. Rueben was seated at the other table.

The food came out seamlessly. Everything was delicious and the presentation was appealing and attractive. He'd switched his cocktail to champagne and then to red wine. A Nero D'Avola. It gave him a kick that Kamaru was getting into wine in such a big way. He remembered back when they used to sit on a stoop in D.C. He was visiting Kamaru in college. They'd sit on his stoop and drink forties out of paper bags and talk shit. A lot of times, Rueben was with them too. Kamaru was with Claire, as ever, but most of that time, Rome and Rueben had been single.

"You boys some dogs," Kamaru would say. They'd all three laugh.

"Grass is always greener. I'm sure it's nicer how you got it set up, Kam," Rome told him.

"Speak for yourself, bro. I'm out here having a blast," Rueben laughed some more.

"You looking for something more steady, Romey-Rome?" Kamaru asked.

"I'm not rushing anything. But I think it could be nice. Nice to give it a shot."

The rehearsal dinner came to a close. Kamaru and Claire stood at the end of the room again, arms around each other's waists, thanking everyone, telling them all how special they were to be in their lives. Some touching stuff. Rome pursed his lips, proud of his friend, knowing this was one of those real and good things to experience in one's life.

They said goodbye to the old timers and the younger crowd assembled, agreeing to meet at the bar Claire and her girlfriends loved to do karaoke at.

"You gonna go up, Rome?" Claire asked him, her arms around his neck as they stood at the bar. "You gotta do one for me. I'm getting married tomorrow!"

"Guess I have to then, huh?" he said, and kissed her on the cheek.

He signed up and when his name was called, Claire and all her girlfriends came up to the stage and clapped and hollered and danced for him. They made him look better than he was. When he finished, they all cheered like he was a rock star.

He went up to the bar after to get another drink. As he waited for his order, Rueben came up beside him.

"Looks like you still got it," he said to Rome.

Rome's drink arrived just in time. He took it and brought it up to his lips right after he said, "Guess so."

"It's good to see you. Seems like you're doing well," Rueben said.

"Thanks. Hope you're well too, Rueben."

Rome left him standing there and walked over to Claire's table. He took a seat. She was talking to her friend, but she looked at him worriedly and gave him a questioning thumbs up. He answered with his own affirmative thumb. She nodded and went back to her conversation.

They closed the bar down. Rome could barely remember getting into an Uber, or sliding his card down the slot to make it into his hotel room, but he woke up and everything was fine. He'd even remembered to put a glass full of water on his nightstand. He rolled over in his bed and sat up and drank all of it right away.

He got a ride to the wedding the next day with the couple he'd sat with at the rehearsal dinner. He felt good about the suit he wore and when he arrived to the wedding, he got a lot of compliments. Looking sharp! Mr. *GQ*! It felt weird to receive those compliments as single unit, as an individual, when it used to be something else.

The ceremony was beautiful, everything he was sure Claire could've wanted. And what Kamaru wanted too, because he'd attained that ultimate level of pure love, where you just wanted your partner to be happy no matter what. Rome clapped as loud as he could when the reverend said kiss the bride. Someone next to him said, "Man, that was it. That's what you want from a wedding." Rome nodded, smiling big.

The party made its way to the reception. The food was buffet style. An old friend and Rome snuck out to the parking lot to swig whiskey, smoke weed. Claire smushed a slice of cake into Kam's face. Everyone was having a ball.

Rome was at the bar, waiting on a proper drink. Rueben appeared next to him. Rome looked over to him, sort of drunk.

"Pretty good wedding," Rueben said.

"Yeah," Rome answered.

"I'm sorry, man. About back then. It was selfish of me. Stupid of me. I thought I was in love with her."

Rome didn't have anything to say. He stood there, leaning against the bar, his mouth sort of open.

"I thought she loved me too. We both made a big mistake."

"OK," Rome said, holding himself against the bar, needing the bar.

"Do you think we could be friends again?" Rueben asked.

Rome hadn't stopped looking at him, the whole time. Listened to every word. Accepted every word.

Finally, he said, "Nah, I'm good."

His drink arrived and he tipped and walked away. He went outside the place. He sat on a ledge.

After a while, Kamaru had come up to him. Sat beside him. Rome looked over. Sort of a silly expression on his face. Sort of amused.

"Saw you and Rueben talking."

"Yeah," Rome said.

"Y'all bury the hatchet?" he asked.

"He wanted to. I declined."

"Damn. Really? He came up to you right? Apologized?"

"Yeah," Rome said.

"So why not? Why not forgive him? Why not be the bigger man?"

"'Cause fuck him. And fuck her. And fuck it." Rome laughed. Then he raised his glass. "Congratulations, brother."

I LOVE YOUR HAIR

Denise was a beautiful woman who had a Russian mom and a dad from Ethiopia. Her skin was perfect. Mahogany, like the grained wood of some custom-made furniture you'd find in a five star hotel. Her lips looked like they belonged on a billboard. And her hair, her huge hair, it was better than a crown. Better than a halo even. Any time she walked into a room, more than half the people would stop whatever they were doing, stop and just regard her in awe. She was a real sight. And we were in Austin, Texas. Absolutely no one looked like her. So of course, I felt very proud walking around with her, taking her out to eat, whatever. I knew nothing romantic was ever going to happen, and I knew why, and she most definitely knew also. But that didn't mean anyone else did. And she knew she was granting me that mystique.

"You think they think we're dating?" she asked one night when I took her to eat at the fancy restaurant I was working at.

I looked around and saw some of the female employees staring at me, smirking with petty intent. I felt wealthy. But still, I pretended not to see them.

"Nah," I gave Denise a wink. The one I'd been working on my whole life. She shook her head and looked at the menu.

One of the girls who I worked with came by at some point. She said hello and asked if everything was all right and we said everything was.

"I love your hair," she told Denise.

Denise rolled her eyes and looked back at her plate. "Thanks," she managed.

My coworker glanced at me, embarrassed, but not knowing why, and walked away. I was embarrassed too. I didn't know either. I got a little upset. I kept my tone low.

"What was that about?"

"I'm sick of that shit."

"Sick of what shit?"

"What do you mean what shit? White people telling me about my hair. Every. Single. Time. Like there's no other quality they can remark on."

"But you have magnificent hair. You have really, really amazing hair," I said, sort of stunned.

"You don't get it," Denise said, picking up some sashimi with her chopsticks.

"What don't I get? I used to have a pretty nice head of hair myself once upon a time. You've seen pictures."

Denise started laughing. I laughed a little too, but I was also sad my hair was gone. Because I meant that statement. I'd taken my hair for granted and now it was gone and I missed it more than any woman I'd ever known.

"Levy, it's not just about the hair. I don't know how exactly to explain it to you. But I've lived with this my whole life. I know I'm different. I love that I'm different. But I don't like how I'm treated differently. I'm not some specimen. I'm not a creature in a zoo, to be gawked at. Or even worse, I'm not part of a petting zoo. Do you know how many people come up and just try to touch me? Sometimes not even with permission? Put their hand in my hair? Like they don't believe it's real? Like they don't believe I'm real? How would that make you feel?" she said, exasperated.

I scanned the room, but with my hand sort of over my eyes.

I was scared people would be looking at us. We were the only brown people in the restaurant at the moment. I couldn't help but think like that sometimes, notice these things. In my mind, I almost immediately crossed her off as being dramatic. I just wanted her to calm down. Not make a scene. Not this sort of scene. I liked other kinds of scenes. I liked when the both of us would laugh loud and clap our hands, showcase excessive joy. Showcase we were having a better time than everyone else, that we were more attractive or charismatic or interesting. But I didn't want to look like we had problems. I didn't want to look like everyone else.

I was able to smooth it out, get us dessert, and coast out of there. As we were on our way to the door, I saw Dohlar at my right, setting a table. His hands were moving plates and glasses but his glittering green cat eyes were on us and he was grinning like he knew a secret. As we passed, he gave me a wink. It was good but not as good as mine. I flicked him off as we left, a smile on my face.

■

Days later, I was at work, second shift in a row. I was in the middle of my work week. That always meant something different in the service industry. My weekend was all over the place, rarely went together, and could change at a moment's notice. My only thing, really, was I didn't want to work both Friday and Saturday together. I hated the kinds of people who went out on the weekends. But I also hated going out on the weekends and being around those people in my free time. Flip of the coin, I guess. Might as well make some money off them, but still of the utmost importance to preserve the soul.

I had this table of sweet women, white women, about my

mother's age, maybe older. It was one of their birthdays. They were having a ball. I got along with them fine and enjoyed the time we got to converse. I wish I could've spent more time with them, but it was busy as hell. It was always busy as hell in that place.

"Who do you remind me of?" one the ladies asked.

"I don't know, who?" I asked her back. I was projecting joviality, but I'd played this game before and it disappointed me to have to play it now, because I'd actually been having a good time with these ladies. I guess it was this thing where I felt, hey, this is nice, you ladies are a breath of fresh air from the pretentious dipshits that typically frequent this place. But now, you too, want to lump me into something familiar. Which was human nature, of course. The need to find a way to relate something, so you can connect. So you can see that the worlds aren't so far apart. "I know that thing! See! We're not so different!"

But we sometimes we just are.

I used to be asked that question all the time, back when I had hair. "Who do you remind me of?" Working at this restaurant in Virginia, still in college. The moms loved me then too. They always loved me, after the initial stage. After they found out how articulate I was. That they were safe with me. That I'd take care of them. That's all they really wanted. That wasn't wrong. I understood.

Back then, with my big black curly hair, the comparison was always Lenny Kravitz. Now, honestly, I love Lenny Kravitz. However, I looked nothing at all, in the least bit, like Lenny Kravitz.

So here I was again but with no hair, no chance at Lenny. The rest of the women looked at their friend, awaiting her answer along with me, awaiting the identity of my doppelgänger.

"Cuba! Cuba Gooding Jr! Oh my God, I loved *Jerry McGuire*!" she exclaimed.

Now, in the base of my heart, I truly believed she was trying to pay some kind of pleasant compliment. I smiled, smiled big, thinking about giving her my patented wink, then deciding, realizing, I no longer had the energy. That doing so would deplete me for the rest of the evening. So I pursed my lips, nodded, and walked away. I prayed someone at her table shook her head in embarrassment. I'd never find out. Fuck a twenty percent tip.

■

There was a new cocktail bar that had opened up in downtown. I told Denise about it and asked her to meet me there. She was never on time. I was super punctual, always, but I'd figured out not everyone lived by my rules. That sounds very simple but in fact is an extremely difficult and sometimes painful lesson to learn. Anyway, regarding Denise, I did that thing where I told her to meet me somewhere thirty minutes before I actually got there, knowing even still she'd manage to get there late. That afternoon, it was by fifteen minutes. Sometimes the predictability of a thing, even when it frustrates you initially, can provide some measure of comfort when you begin to see it in its truth and so readily come to accept it has nothing to do with you. It's just the nature of a thing.

I ordered a Last Word with mezcal and she ordered some kind of champagne cocktail. It was a very pretty drink, and she looked like a million bucks drinking it.

I sat there watching her, a smile on my face.

"Why don't we date, Denise?" I asked her. "I'm the only one who gets you."

I just threw it out there, like it was nothing. Like I'd never shot a basketball before. Not once in my life. I even smiled when I said it.

Denise laughed. Her head went all the way back. Me and the rest of the bar stared at her brown neck.

"You don't get me. None of you motherfuckers do."

"What don't I get?"

"I wouldn't know where to start. I really wouldn't." She looked around. The bar had suddenly gotten crowded. It wasn't late at all. A big group had infiltrated the small bar. This part of town had dumb shit going on like bar crawls for start-up companies that wanted to build team morale, though these kinds of activities only really exposed people's vices further and more rapidly than they may have wished for. I could see it a mile off, and knew it was time for us to leave.

"We should go," I told Denise.

I paid our tab and we stood and weaved our way out of there. The bar had been dark and when we opened the door the sunlight felt like an attack. Denise stepped out first.

A group of men met us. Sizing up their choice in clothing, grooming, and body language, we could decipher quickly they were a group of young gay white men, ready to enjoy the weekend. Indeed, I forgot at the time it was Friday. The one weekend night I had off this week.

As our companies met at the door, something incredible happened.

Through their chatter, just as my vision was returning from the blinding flash of the sun, the man forefront of the group—a small man with a smart haircut, both sides of his head shaved, the front combed up sharp, pink V-neck, high shorts, white teeth—his face expressing complete wonder at Denise's beauty or height or whatever, he reached with one hand, no word uttered, for her hair. Just like that. Not with any aggression, similar almost to the innocence of a child's curiosity. And what Denise did: she smacked his hand aside. And what he did: reached again with his other hand, seamlessly, like nothing at all had happened to the first. And she smacked this hand too. Thwarted, she then really lit into him.

I honestly don't know what she said. She was fury. All fury. Their whole group appeared sincerely baffled. As if they were the victims of some aggressor from another country, scolding them in a foreign language, they not knowing the words but understanding dire consequences were imminent. Not knowing why or for what, only that they were in it now. These consequences had always existed in the world and it was their mistake for walking straight into that arrogant ignorance. Yet it still remained unbelievable to them. They couldn't fathom this might become their immediate reality. Maybe you've never had someone accuse you of something you never in a million years thought you could do. I knew what that felt like though.

They tried to explain themselves to her. And as they did, to my astonishment, I watched as their faces began to melt off, and their true faces revealed themselves to us: reptilian lizard faces, gawking and appalled that they'd been rooted out.

I swayed on my heels, losing my shit.

Denise grabbed my wrist and pulled me ahead. We both started running. I couldn't really see, my vision had suddenly blitzed, all I could do was follow.

"Here! Take this!" she yelled back at me.

She put something into my hand. It was the hilt of a sword. It felt heavy in my grip, weighed my arm down. The blade fell to the concrete of the sidewalk. I was going to have to hold it with two hands if I was going to swing it. Where the hell did Denise get this thing? I looked up at her. Her back was to me. I could see, in front of her, a woman was marching towards her, her hands up.

"Your hair! Your hair! Your hair!" the woman said, like a doll from the eighties, the kind you pull the string from.

Denise, in perfect ninja form, lunged forward, crouched, and cleaved the woman perfectly in half.

The top half lay on the sidewalk, hands still reaching for Denise's glorious hair, an expression of ecstasy permanently stamped on her dissolving lizard face.

"Holy shit!" I yelled.

They were coming out in droves then. Coming from everywhere. Hordes. I started cutting everything that came close to me, sobbing and yelling at the same time, half the time with my eyes closed. There were so many. They wanted Denise's hair. They wanted our skin. They wanted the way we talked and danced and laughed and the way we held each other and the way we clapped and the way we cried and got mad and raised our voices and kept silent and the way we walked and ran and made food and mourned and made music and sang songs and held our brothers and sisters and sons and daughters and nieces and nephews and uncles and aunts. I collapsed. There were too many. I thought I was going to die. I really thought I was going to die. They were all over me. They smothered me. I was waiting for one of them to clamp their teeth down on my neck and tear the life out of me. *My life.*

And in an instant, they were all ripped from me. A flame washed over me, the heat singeing my brown skin. I blinked, staring up, my back on the street, clear from the horde. Denise stood above me, still holding her blade, except now, her blade was on fire. She stood over me, her expression brave, unwavering. She was not afraid.

"Let's go. Stay close. Trust me," she said.

"I promise," I told her.

CRAWFISH SEASON

I got off from my dumb job in the afternoon and did some meager grocery shopping and when I got home, I sat down at the desk and started punching into the keys. I was working on something new. I only had the screen to look at. There wasn't anything else in the room besides the boxes I hadn't unpacked and my mattress and box spring on the floor.

I did what I could and when I finished, I went downstairs and across the street into the Milan.

If I'm solo, I always go to the end of the bar. And even there, I might not always find peace. A woman appeared, like a bill I'd forgotten to pay, purring lowly into my left ear.

"Whenever I come in here and I go to the end of the bar, it's because I don't want to talk to anybody or 'cause I need to charge my phone. So I'm wondering, stud, which one is it for you?"

"Both," I told her.

She faded off. I stuck around for a few boilermakers, asked for the tab, shook my bartender's hand, and scooted on out.

Outside, a man with a handlebar mustache and mullet was leaning against a white pickup, smoking a cigarette.

"Hey, bud. You hungry?"

"Huh?" I said.

"Got crawfish. Fresh from a boil and still hot. Over four pounds. Knock out some for me."

He opened up a dirty white ice cooler. A mound of crawfish glowed red in there like treasure.

"Free?"

"I ain't got no cash register."

I could've been suspicious. Instead, I got on in there. He was right. They were still hot. And they were damn good. I snapped them up and sucked them out. Snagged some mushrooms and a sausage too. He just stood there, smoking, saying nothing, staring out into the dark like it wasn't dark at all. Like he could see just fine.

After I had my fill, he handed me a dirty rag from the bed of his truck. I wiped my hands.

"Let me buy you a drink," I said.

"I ain't drinking this month."

"God bless you," I told him.

"I could use it," he said solemnly.

I put my hand on his shoulder and he nodded to me. I walked back up the stairs to my place, unlocked and relocked the door. I took a seat in my chair, trying to look into my apartment like that man had been looking into the darkness. Like I could see me out there, out in the world, and I was doing OK. Like I was happy.

Well. I was back in New Orleans.

A COOL CUCUMBER

I worked with this guy. He was a real nice guy. Fresh from out of town. Tall, handsome, long blond hair. A real babe magnet. He was married. Weird for a young guy. A lot of us couldn't wait to see who she was. I guess we had big expectations. It wasn't fair but most of us were pretty judgmental. Jaded. Still running around being assholes.

Sometimes the new guy would give me rides to work. He wanted to fit in, and I took advantage of that the same way it'd been done to me and all before me and all to come. He drove a used Civic hatchback, paint job chipping, muffler loud as fuck. I didn't care. I liked attention. Especially if it was disruptive.

"My wife is coming in to eat tonight," the new guy told me.

"Fuck yeah. With who?"

"Solo."

"We'll roll out the red carpet, baby."

The staff got ready for the night. We went over the specials in detail and practiced pitches, discussed specific guests with specials needs, big parties, what time the pops would come, and our last reservation of the night. Tish gave a quick presentation on a new Loire Valley wine we'd added.

The night came as furious as ever. And the team was tight. Completely prepared. We were like a pirate crew. Everyone was certain. Everyone knew the hit of the tide and how to roll with it. We all felt like killers. So even if we weren't best friends, we felt like we knew each other better than best friends, in a different but still intimate way. Because, and I realized how dramatic it is to say it like this, it felt like our lives were on the line. The margin of error was so small. No one wanted to be the weak link. The weak link didn't last long here. We had to all be completely dependable. The money was the best some of us would ever make in our lives. That's why it was so damn hard to leave.

"My wife's at table ten," the new guy said giddily into my ear as I was putting my order in.

I looked over. I sized her up quickly, like you do in our business. She checked out. Thin nose, black hair styled like she'd jumped straight out from a pinup calendar, a blouse that showed her arms plastered with tattoos, and plenty of cleavage, but not in a distasteful way. But it was a lot. Yeah, the new guy was a certified stud, but she was something else. And she knew it.

We were introduced. I took her hand and repeated my name. She didn't say a word. She didn't have to. Maybe that was the point.

She was only shown the drink menu. The food was going to just be sent out. We did this often for people who came in to eat. Usually only for people with big, big money. We'd sort of become known for it. A group would sit down and the spokesperson would say, "We know we're supposed to trust you, here are some things we know we want, here are some things we'd like to stay away from. Send us food until we tell you to stop." Nine times out of ten we'd blow them out of the water. I could see the allure. The delight in surprise. Decadence. And we were confident. Because we knew how good our product was. The size of the bill that would come out at the end could look like a month of rent.

So it paid to have friends like us, or even better, a significant other, because we also had the power to cancel out the bill. We gave his wife the red carpet. Everyone came over to introduce themselves at some point, dropping off food, describing them in full and articulate detail, and she was a cool cucumber with every one of us. Not snobby. Just a touch of the ice queen. I didn't take it any bad sort of way. She didn't owe me shit.

A couple hours went by. The restaurant was slowly starting to chill out. She was ending like a champion. A seared sliver of foie gras on a warm ball of nigiri assisted by a glass of Sauternes. Bliss. Her eyes fluttered. Beautiful eyelashes. The moment in *The Matrix* where the program causes the tiny explosion between the woman's legs. I almost felt perverted for watching this exact moment with the guest, but it was a moment you wanted to relive as many times as possible while you were still on this green Earth.

I was at the bar picking up something when his wife was on her way out. They hugged at the door. She saw me over his shoulder. She gave me a cool nod and breezed out. Light as a feather.

"She have a good time?" I asked the new guy.

"Blew her mind."

We high-fived. I could tell how proud he was. And he ought to be. I was happy for him. In a lot of ways.

It was the end of the night and we were finishing up, doing our side work. We sat next to each other, polishing silverware. Joanie was vacuuming at the end of the restaurant, a strangely comforting buzz. The sushi guys were cleaning their station, wrapping up the fish, wiping down their cutting boards. Mitch was behind the bar, taking inventory. A tranquility had settled over the restaurant.

"How did y'all meet?" I asked the new guy.

"I was visiting Seattle. That's where she was living at the time. Working in a bar. I was in a hostel next door. We hit it off. I ended up staying there for weeks just to be around her. I was probably pretty annoying at first, but she finally said yes to a date. Things kept growing. I persuaded her to travel to Hawaii with me somehow. That's where we got married."

"That's crazy. Sounds like it happened fast."

"It did. I was surprised myself. I just didn't want anything else. I couldn't imagine being somewhere without her with me. I'm really lucky."

There was a way he said it, how honest he was maybe, that made me feel real sad for him. I couldn't figure out why that was.

So all I said was, "Jeez. That's great, man."

■

Another day, another dollar. We got through service. The new guy was really taking to it fast. He was a quick learner. Which was really great in this environment. This wasn't a good place for someone to have to tell you something more than twice.

"Feel like grabbing a drink after work?"

I knew he'd say no. He wasn't really a drinker. He wasn't really a bar type either. He liked to go to the gym after work. He worked out a lot. He was sort of a health freak. He was very popular with the ladies who dined in the restaurant. He'd always be popular.

"Nah, man. Thanks though. You know me. Gonna hit the gym before the wife gets home."

"She works this late?"

"A lot more lately. New job."

The manager came by and handed us our tips for the night. I took the large wad of cash and shoved it in my pocket without counting. I folded my polishing rag, standing up. I slapped the new guy on his broad back.

"Have a good night, amigo."

"You going out?"

"Gotta howl, baby."

"Go get 'em."

I went to my bar. I probably went to this bar five nights out of the week. It wasn't on my side of town but the truth was I had no business being on my side of town in the first place, and all the neighbors knew it. I tried to make it so that I only slept over there and a lot of nights I didn't even make it to do that. I wasn't doing a lot of good with all the money I was making, which of course would be something I'd regret the rest of my life. But hey, can't take it with you right? Why pay off some student loans when I could sit at a bar with a bunch of dipshits, drink Budweiser, and shout at people I'd never meet through a television screen?

But the truth was, I was beginning to understand I was wasting my life. It was the same group of us almost every night, hunkered over the counter, and if any of us were ever missing, we were almost jealous. They had to be doing something important not to be here, right? It'd come to feel like we were just at another job. The job after the job. And none of us realized we could just go home. We could just do something else. Sleep. Save our money. Build a shelf. Write a book.

I took a shot of whiskey. A couple walked into the bar. I knew them both. Only one of them surprised me.

The guy came up to me right away. He was a regular too. Younger than me. A pretty enthusiastic fella. I liked him fine. We shook hands.

"Hey, bud, how you doing tonight?"

"I'm doing, brother. I'm doing."

I was looking past him to the girl. He must've picked up on that.

"This is my girlfriend. Wanda, this is Levy."

"Hi, Levy," Wanda said monotone. We shook hands.

This time, she did say her name. Different than before. Of course, this was a different kind of meeting than before, and we both knew it. This time, I was quiet. I just stared at her. She bit her full ruby lip, ever so slightly.

"You just hanging out tonight, Lev?"

"Yeah, man. You see it."

"Word. Well, we're gonna grab a drink. Maybe we'll join you."

"Yeah. Sure, hoss."

They went to the middle of the bar where Crow was making some drinks. My friend stood there chatting with him. Wanda looked back at me and gave me that cool nod once again.

I left a little while later. They were outside smoking. I didn't act rushed or anything. I said adios to them as I passed by, my hand up. He waved. I got another nod from her. A real cool cat. Totally composed. I don't know if you could be taught that. She was that good.

I went back to my side of town and had a hard time getting to sleep, but I finally did.

The next day at work, the new guy was in there early, stocking. When he saw me, he gave me dap. Our hands smacking together sounded good in an empty restaurant.

"How'd last night go?" he asked me.

"It went. You?"

"It was good. Was at the gym for a couple hours. My old lady ended up just crashing at a co-workers. She was out so late working."

"Huh," I said.

"She's a hard worker. Maybe works too hard. I hope we can go on vacation soon. She deserves one."

"Yeah," I said, rubbing my chin.

"You OK, Levy?" he asked me.

I looked up at him. He was a lot taller than me. A lot younger too. Fresh face, full of optimism and hope. I realized he still had plenty of time. I nodded to him.

"Yeah, I'm good. Let me get started on side work."

He smiled and turned back to stocking the wine. I sighed, then I draped my black button up on the back of a chair and started setting up the restaurant.

THE WEEKEND

I finished my cigarette and flicked it out into the street. I watched the embers fade away like a comet sizzling into the ether. I always came into work through the back door at night. I didn't mind taking the front in the day. When the bar was calm. I always found it soothing to walk into a dark bar when the sun was still up. But at night, it would all be chaos, and I'd rather not see with my own eyes what sort of madness I was walking into.

I could hear it before I even opened the door, and when I did open it, the clamor spiked to a deafening level immediately. The way the heat hit me was like the sun was blowing a kiss onto my face. Scores of people waiting impatiently at the bar all fixed their deranged eyes onto me, and I beheld them with zero emotion. I hadn't even clocked in yet. I invoked the stoic demeanor of a prison guard. I wasn't going to give any of these people shit just yet.

Not for a little longer.

The bar was fully staffed. Weekends weren't for newbies. Make no mistake, shifts like these were pure war. But different people wore it in different ways. War wasn't for everyone.

I loved watching Dave. Maybe for sadistic reasons. He was a big boy and for some reason he was popular, but whenever the night really began to cook, all the chuckles quit and then you could see the fear of God in his eyes. His shirt betrayed that further as it became soaked through by how much he was sweating. We would never say anything, of course, we weren't children. After all, a person can't control how much they perspire. But it was in the spastic movement, the face as it barely held check. It was all there to see. One slip, and it could all come tumbling down. Dave was a panicked man, maybe he always had been, and panic was easy to spread.

But luckily for him, he wasn't with a crew that fell into fear.

The hungry hordes were there for certain, frothing from the mouth, eyeballs crazed because if they didn't get this drink and get it back to their table in time the world would surely end. But the gladiators were there to defend the bar, with their lives if need be. These were the ones that bore the scars, most of them invisible. You could see it all if you just stopped to watch them work. It was like ballet, but more metal. A mixture of chess and boxing. Their eyes were open, fixed on a point, but still they saw everything, and their limbs moved in such a way it appeared as if they were summoning an element from the earth and bending it to their will, all to form something drawn entirely from their recollection. Pure finesse. Inspiring to witness. It was the reason why the confident bartender would always get complimented, tipped well, and laid.

The Rain stood there, giving the double shake, both hands in unison, his pose the very same that it had been for the last decade, and when he did so, his gaze reached beyond the bar, beyond the frenzy, to some place far away, maybe some place he hoped to visit one day, places like Costa Rica, Fiji, or Milwaukee. He poured the drink into a coupe, right up to the lip, a lemon peel waiting for the final touch. Maybe no one would care for such a little thing in the maelstrom of a night like this, but I saw, and I knew. I was in class and the tuition was my life.

I caught Tito's eye and Tito winked at me and never missed his stride, gliding like he was on a pair of roller skates. Don't get me wrong, he had a sheen of perspiration on his brow as well, there was just a difference between him and Dave. The difference was: he made it look good. One curl hanging down just above his right eye, the quick easy smile like a winning gun in the Wild West. He was at home in the chaos. He lived for it.

And Irene, our Dark Queen, at the end, holding down the turn of the tide, the most oppressive end of the bar, where even the sharks sank. But it was as if she knew the fish were really only in an aquarium, and she was on the outside looking in, so they could never really harm her. She was in control. And if the fish ever got too unruly, all she had to do was scoop them up and flush them down the toilet. Irene was sheer composure, a fantasy, our rock.

Our red-headed, red-bearded boss came stumbling out from the back room looking like he'd just shaken himself out of slumber like some hibernating grizzly. He did have broad shoulders; it wasn't a bad comparison. Without looking or talking to any of us, he began to line up shot glasses on the back bar, like totems to ward off the evil in the world. He snatched up some clandestine bottle of dark liquor and, holding it upside down, filled the glasses up. Then he took a cowbell, yes a cowbell, from a hidden cubby hole and banged hell from it.

All of us paused in our actions and heeded the call like automatons commanded, ambling over to where the shot glasses twinkled. The crowds of people waiting to receive their drink orders watched us, appalled and powerless. Once we had all gathered, our boss somberly, dutifully, lifted one of the glasses, and we each took our own and raised them similarly, traditionally. He had this glint in his eye, our captain, and the glint reminded us that this was just a night and we were just getting drunk and so were they and they would go on with their lives or maybe they wouldn't, but that in this place, that night, we would live, we had nothing to fear, nothing could kill us, the night was ours, and so was their money. Even Dave chilled the fuck out for that amber second. We took the shots back. I howled like a damn demon. Everybody grinned. Then we got back to work.

THE STOOP

Freddie stood behind his dirty screen door, staring out onto the street. Bunch of quiet. Everybody's inside, Freddie thought. Where they oughta be, unless they had a pool. It was summertime. Way too hot. All it did was make people crazy. But really, he knew the real reason why the street was empty. These were the new days.

He shook the cubes of ice in his Crown and Seven, his long black fingers curling around the glass like spider legs. He toed open the screen door, all matted with dirt and pollen, and stepped out onto his stoop.

He was in the shadow of his shotgun but even so the humidity wrapped around him thick. With a lot of grunting, clutching on the rail, he slowly lowered his butt down to take a seat.

"Ooh," he said.

The stairs, once a vibrant green, were dusty and faded and chipping bad. He looked to the right, next door to him. That house had been boarded up for years now. Vines grew all over it and the boards that were nailed to the windows bore faded spray paint. On the roof, flowers bloomed. Somebody might mistake them for being pretty, but he knew they were weed flowers, so he didn't like them.

Sometimes, he had a hard time remembering who used to live there. At last he would recall. Danny Wheeler and his family. He hadn't any inkling as to where they'd ended up. He wished one day they would just reappear, car pulling a trailer, all kinds of stuff pressed up on the windows. He wondered if he'd recognize

Danny's kids. If they would recognize him. I don't look so much different, Freddie thought to himself. He took a grip of his belly fat. He took another sip from his drink.

He heard a door push open a few doors down and across the street. One of the houses getting all the repair in the past months. Heavy renovation. Brand new paint. Bars on the windows. Freddie would bet a shot of Old Granddad the floors were glossier than a motherfucker. All that repair, and he hadn't recognized a single soul. Coming out of the door, a pale man with straw hair holding a briefcase. His head leaned down on his shoulder and a cell phone was lodged between. Freddie could just barely hear him talking. The man locked the door behind him, then the screen door, before stepping down onto the sidewalk. He walked up the block, towards Freddie. As he passed Freddie, he smiled and held up a hand. Freddie stared at the man hard and returned no motion. The man got into a shiny car and started it and drove away.

Freddie lingered on his stoop about a half an hour longer. The only other person to pass was a young boy on a bike, shirtless, onyx skin glistening in the sun. It was a very nice bicycle the boy rode. Freddie didn't waste any time wondering about stuff like that anymore. He got back up with some grunting and went back into his house to make himself another Crown and Seven. Maybe play a record or two.

■

A white and black taxicab cruised down the wrecked street of the neighborhood at a leisurely pace. A dumb glossy beetle bumping along. When it stopped, a young woman stepped out. Blond hair, the ends pink. She wore a backpack and pulled a rolling suitcase behind her. The cab left. She looked up and down the block, smiling. Down the block, she saw an older black man sitting on a stoop holding a glass. He was staring back at her. He stood up slowly, holding onto a rail, and returned to his house. Now she was completely alone. She stepped up the stoop, took some more looks up and down the block, and picked out a key from the soil of a hanging flower pot. The door was a bright purple. The window shutters were yellow. She almost laughed. She unlocked the door to the house and stepped inside. The air conditioning was running and the lights were off but she could see from the light coming through the blinds that there was a note on the table, just as she'd been informed. She closed the door behind her, locking it.

■

That first afternoon in town, the young woman discovered a coffee shop just a few blocks away from the house she was staying in. It didn't take her long to fall into conversation with people. She'd always been easy to talk to. Her parents loved to tell stories of her walking up to complete strangers in airports and striking up conversations. It had carried on into her adult life, though of course she'd had to become more cautious.

She was gathering information about the neighborhood. Off of a recommendation, she checked out Frenchmen Street later that evening. It was a weekday but there were enough people out to warrant walking in the streets. Food and music filled the air. Open guitar cases with dollar bills and coins. People sipping from to-go cups and makeshift tables for street poets and their typewriters. She stepped into a bar to listen in on a band. She applauded with everyone when they finished a set. A bearded fellow came by with an empty coffee can afterwards and a smile on his face. She added a couple of dollars to it. He gave her a small bow.

New Orleans is so charming, she texted a friend back home.

She didn't stay out too late, still tired from the flight, but the next morning she returned to the coffee shop. The place had some real characters. One of them: a young cute guy from Omaha she'd talked to the previous day. He had a habit of breaking into song whenever he deemed appropriate. It embarrassed her terribly at first, but hardly anyone seemed to turn a head when it kept happening, so she assumed they were all already quite used to his antics. After the third song, he invited her to watch him play later that night. He made her laugh and she was winging the trip anyway, so yeah, sure, she told him. She'd come by.

She was on the phone texting her mother how much fun she was having as she turned onto her temporary block. As she did, she saw the older black man she'd seen the first day, pulling a large ladder off his truck. He seemed to be struggling. She rushed up to help him with the opposite end. His eyes met hers with suspicion initially, but once he settled on her intent, the look relented. He wiped his brow and muttered, "Appreciate ya."

He unlocked a wonky door and they hobbled through a narrow alleyway on the side of his shotgun, into the backyard. They set the ladder up against a tiny Tim Burton shed. In the yard, near the back entrance, there was a life size statue of an angel. The eyes had no pupils. Freddie wiped his brow again and put his hand to his hip, exhaling, staring at the ground. The young woman chewed her bottom lip, standing there.

"Care for an iced tea or a beer?" he asked her.

It was hardly past noon.

"Sure. I'll take a beer," she said.

They sat on the stoop, drinking a couple of High Lifes. "I'm Freddie," he said.

"Andrea. Nice to meet you, Freddie."

She shook the hand he held out. She could feel the bones in his hand. "Likewise."

"I'm visiting," she told him.

"Oh, I figured as much."

"You lived here long, Freddie?"

"All my life."

They drank their beer, looking out on the street. A car passed by, bobbing along. Their beer bottles sweat onto their laps.

"Do you do carpentry, Freddie?"

"Yeah. Stuff like that."

"My dad's kind of a handy man."

"Oh yeah?" Freddie said.

"Yeah. The last house we lived in, where my parents retired, it was this big house that had all these things wrong with it. My dad called it a fixer-upper. I was just a kid, so of course I thought it was a pile of junk. It was just an old house. But being retired, my dad had all this time to actually fix it up. He liked the work and in the end did a great job. Everyone on the block could see the difference. So instead of hiring other people, they asked him. Can you do this, can you do that. I guess he got kind of famous. On the block anyway. I bet you're kind of famous around here, huh?"

"Naw. I just know people," Freddie said, tipping his beer back.

They sat there some moments longer, drinking their beers. Andrea finished and thanked Freddie for it.

"I'll be your neighbor for the rest of the week. That house right there. Doing the Airbnb thing."

"Is that what they calling all that?" Freddy asked.

"The houses you can rent. From owners. Yeah."

"From owners. Huh."

"A lot cheaper than hotels and you get to be in the cool

neighborhoods. It's pretty great." She stood up. "So I'll see you around, right, Freddie?"

"Guess so," he said.

She waved as she walked back to her house. Freddie nodded.

■

Freddie was watching that boy riding his bicycle again. He wondered where the other kids were. He didn't wonder long. He remembered himself as a kid, playing in the streets. Playing stickball. Playing till the sun came down. His uncle barbequing. Mom and aunt and sisters on the stoop, talking and talking. Music up loud, no one seemed to mind, it was just how it was, as natural as cicadas. His older brother had just bought a new car. He'd wash it every Sunday. Gave Freddie a beating that one time he hit it playing stickball, right in front of everyone. But Freddie knew he'd deserved it. He knew he'd hit the car on purpose. He loved his older brother.

At least once a day that week, Andrea would catch Freddie sitting on that stoop, staring off. She'd approach him gingerly and he'd blink, lost in some childlike reverie, and then he'd nod to her and she'd sit down and maybe he'd say something about what he was looking at but mostly he did not.

"It's my last night," Andrea told him. "Going to a big show on St. Claude. The music here has really been so great. We just don't have it like this at home."

"It's special here. In New Orleans. Always has been."

"Man. To have grown up here. I bet that was really something. All the things you've seen come along," Andrea said.

He sat there a long time after she left. It was that time of year. The sun was taking longer to come down.

Freddie was really tying one on that night. He was playing his records loud. He knew he didn't have to care about anybody complaining. Not as long as they didn't 'bnb ole Danny's place. He took a swig of his plastic cap whiskey and chased it with a freshly popped can of beer. He stomped his feet, stumbled through his house, pacing, looking at the framed pictures on his wall like he hadn't seen them in years. He felt like everyone was right on the verge of being with him again. He waited for someone to knock on his screen door. He picked up his cordless phone, looking at the numbers, seeing familiar faces rippling in the pool of his mind, just to trickle away. The phone fell from his hand, clattering across his empty dinner table.

He'd fallen asleep with his head in his hand at the dinner table. He'd become some kind of master at being a statue. Just waiting for the pigeons. He could hear someone outside. The candle he'd lit earlier was out but the door was still ajar, just the screen door shut. He stood up, shaky, bracing himself on the chair, scuttling up to the door. From the dark, he peered out into the street from behind the screen.

Down the block he could just make her out. Blondie. Andrea. The street was very dark, but who else could it be. Her hair almost seemed to glow. Freddie nearly smiled.

Then he heard someone else.

"Give me your money, bitch."

Freddie could tell the man was young. Maybe wasn't even a man yet. But he couldn't see anything besides Andrea. Could only see her turn around and put her hands up. He saw the man step from the shadows, his arm held up, pointing something at her. Freddie didn't need to guess what. She handed over her purse. He lowered the hand holding the gun, and struck her with the other hand. Freddie could hear the impact. Hear her gasp. The dark figure dashed back into the night. Freddie could hear her sobbing. She'd fallen onto her knees. When she finally stood, she turned around. She was looking towards his direction. Like she could see in the dark. He closed his door as softly as he could, and leaned against the wall, closing his eyes. He noticed the record still spinning on the turntable, the needle long since lifted.

WORLDS WITHIN WORLDS

The chef was looking over the resume, a finger tapping his narrow lips and the barely visible blond mustache above them.

"Pretty good stuff," the chef said. "He moves a lot though. I don't like that. But he's got a couple of James Beard-winning restaurants. You check his references?"

"I did. All good there. Surprisingly," the manager said.

"OK."

"One more thing. He's black," the manager said.

The chef looked up from the resume, eyebrows raised. "Is there some kind of implication being made here?"

The manager cleared her throat. "Nothing negative. Positive actually. It might be in our best interest to consider a little . . . diversity."

"Consider diversity?" the chef repeated.

"If we're just regarding the times, that is."

"Are you saying we don't consider diversity?" the chef asked, dangerously.

"Not saying that at all, Chef. Just making sure we're . . . on the same page," the manager answered strategically.

"Give him a stage," the chef mumbled, tossing the resume and walking away.

"Heard," the manager replied, running her hand through her platinum blond bob.

■

The applicant showed up to work early and his shirt was pressed. He was clean-shaven, wrote down notes in the pre-shift, and asked smart questions. The manager was right. He was black. But he wasn't that black.

Everyone inspected the applicant, some more aggressively than others. It didn't rattle him. Conversation came easy to him. He found a common ground with every potentially new coworker through the brief conversation they engaged in and when that wasn't available, he simply remained quiet and listened. He was professional. He stood straight. He said things like thank you, excuse me, I see, and sir. The chef liked him but wouldn't let that show for at least another couple shifts. It was critical to maintain a stoic façade. And the chef knew he wasn't seeing everything about the applicant just yet. He'd be foolish to think otherwise.

"He seemed pretty on point," the chef admitted to the manager at the end of the night.

"Out on the floor too. Confident in speech. Takes initiative. Definitely understands spatial awareness, opens and pours wine correctly, fell in easy with the guests."

"Back in the kitchen with the staff too. OK. Hire him. Start him as a runner, let him work up. We'll see if he cops an attitude. It'll depend on him how fast he rises."

"Heard," the manager said.

■

He trained with the longest tenured runner for the whole week. Black dude, REAL BLACK. *Night* black. He had thick braids and he was born and raised in New Orleans. His accent was thicker than the humidity in July.

"Your name Fenton?" the dude asked him.

"Yeah."

"Aight, Fenton. Here's three plates. How you gonna hold 'em?"

Fenton put two on his left forearm and held the third in his right hand. His trainer, his name was Rell, scrutinized the positioning with authentic sincerity. Like he was looking at the shape of a sports car. The things that lay under the hood. It endeared him to Fenton. Fenton admired when people took pride in their work, on any level. Rell took a good look, then smacked Fenton's left arm, the one holding the two plates of hot food. Fenton did not drop the plates and his posture remained stable. Rell nodded.

"Table Nine. Pork belly to seat one, octopus seat two, cavatelli seat four."

Fenton turned on a dime, leaving the kitchen to deliver the food. He placed each dish in front of the guest gracefully, sure to be on their literal right side, open handed, just as instructed. He explained the ingredients of each dish quickly but with clear enunciation. He warned the young lady that her plate may be hot so to take caution. He gave a modest bow as he departed the table. He returned to the kitchen and Rell, observing everything, nodded approvingly.

The shift went by like a breeze. It was a fairly busy night but the flow never got jammed up. Fenton and Rell fell into an easy rhythm with each other. It was clear to Rell this wasn't Fenton's first job in a restaurant, having never been informed of Fenton's resume, but all the same, Fenton never acted haughty, didn't act like anything Rell was telling him was a waste of his time. He simply listened to his trainer, did his job clean, and if he had a question, he asked. And Rell, with no seemingly petty territorial claim invested in his job, only expressed one continual reaction through their training shifts.

Relief.

They were both relieved. Fenton was relieved to have a job. Rell was relieved to have someone else around who could do his job and who was competent, thus lightening his workload and freeing him up for shifts he might request off. But those are things most coworkers can't, or won't, say to each other. Very often, these appreciations lay unspoken. But between the lines, through body language and the freedom to execute a task without smothering supervision, a relationship of trust was created. The two of them didn't have to say it. Maybe, just maybe, they could rely on one another.

After their last training shift together, nearly two weeks later, they stood outside, rolling up their aprons neatly. Rell said, "You're new to town."

"I am," Fenton answered, though Rell hadn't asked him a question.

"I'm about to head to reggae night at the Den."

"The Den?"

"Dragon's Den," Rell said, smirking. It was a kind of smirk Fenton liked. He knew it meant bad things but bad in a fun way.

"Is that an invite?" Fenton asked.

Rell shrugged. "Where you stay at?"

"Up Washington from here."

"I'll come swoop you in an hour or something."

Fenton was ready when he arrived. He sent a text that he was outside and when Fenton got in the car, Rell was smirking again.

"Why you move to this neighborhood?"

"I wanted to live by myself. Rent was cheap. It's close to everything."

"Central City. Ha. Yeah, you right," Rell chuckled.

Fenton shrugged in his seat. "I ain't worried."

"Some nights, you might need be."

They cruised through the city dark, streetlights twinkling like a Hype Williams music video. Rell pointed out things to him, and not in any corny way. He pointed them out in an honest way, like they were places he was proud of. And that he'd be honored for Fenton to visit under his recommendation. This is my banh mi spot. This is my wing spot. This is where I go to get a Dark 'n' Stormy.

"You like Dark 'n' Stormys?" Fenton asked.

"I better, if I live here, baby. One way or the other."

Fenton did his best to imprint the spots Rell pointed out into memory. The street names. A big tree that might be in front of the place. How the highway curved over the city just briefly, like an arm around a shoulder.

He also realized he felt an odd appreciation for being called "baby" by another man. It wasn't something Fenton would admit out loud. It was the casualness of it. The nonchalance. Natural, like breathing. The music in the car cranked and Fenton bobbed his head to the beat. Rell passed him a freshly lit blunt. Fenton received it seamlessly and pulled. Whoo, boy. It was good shit. He got high quick and tried not to get scared by that.

Rell parked the car. It seemed too soon for Fenton, but he got out anyway. There was a line but Rell somehow was able to circumvent it. Fenton had cut lines before, but it never ceased feeling cool.

They entered into a cluster of people and that broke out into a long alley and they continued on into the back where a pocket of tall men stood shrouded in shadow, another joint circulating, their gaze imperceptible but still tangible as Rell introduced Fenton and Fenton respectfully but in a low voice said what's up.

The joint passed around twice. Fenton was conservative with

his turn. He didn't talk. He listened. Listened to the gossip, the cadence, the accents. He absorbed them all. Tucked them back into the shelves of his brain cells to use for reference on a later date. He laughed at the right times and was bold enough to say when that appropriate stage of the story emerged, "That nigga wylin'."

He was allowed to become invisible amongst them, which is often the first step to joining the ranks. Unspoken acceptance. The next step was always then to step up when your card got called.

"DJ popping off upstairs," one of them said stoically. Like the weather was overcast outside. The joint disappeared and everyone began to move. Fenton followed them upstairs into a room that may have been large but he'd never know. The bodies that occupied that place were uncountable. The light was a hazy violet and it made everyone there glow like distant stars in outer space. All black people. Fenton didn't see a single white human being. Not to say there weren't any there. Fenton just didn't see any. And simultaneously, he wondered why that observation gave him the unique relief that it did.

To get around, they had to squeeze through a sea of bodies. It wasn't romantic, only necessary, and not personal, unless someone made it personal. It was very hot in the room and the music was very loud. So loud it shook the floor. And the floor shook even more the further in they traveled. The volume of bodies continued to amass the deeper they went. In the center of the room was a ring of people and within the ring, one person dancing, underneath the now vibrant blue light. Fenton got so close he could see the sweat glisten off her galaxy-lit skin.

The dancer had her eyes closed as she spun, her hands above her head, mouth open, teeth white. Her hips jerked like someone was pressing buttons, but still completely fluid. Mesmerizing.

Fenton shook himself from his reverie, and coming out, caught

Rell's gaze upon him. He was doing that smirk again. Fenton shook his head, embarrassed. Rell passed him a newly lit joint. Fenton let the bass and percussion roll over his body. Everyone was there at the same time. No one wanted to leave the vortex.

■

"What do you think?" the chef asked him after he'd tasted the dish. It was intended to be the new fish special. Skate with a lemon emulsion and sautéed ramps. It wasn't going to be cheap and it wasn't supposed to taste cheap.

It was Fenton's first month and the chef was asking him his opinion on the flavor profile of a special his sous chef had presented. The chef and sous chef and Rell all stared at Fenton expectedly.

"It tastes great. There's layers to it. That makes it interesting. I think a touch of citrus and pinch of salt would go a long way. That's just me."

The chef and sous chef looked at each other and the sous chef nodded and went to get a lemon and some sea salt and he added them carefully and they all took another bite. They all looked at each other like they'd discovered gold. Rell's expression was near disbelief. It made Fenton want to laugh but he didn't.

"That's it," the chef said.

"We can put it on the specials board tonight," the sous said.

"Let Beth know, Rell," the chef said.

Everyone shook hands.

During pre-shift, the chef let Fenton explain the special. He stood there with his arms crossed as Fenton did. The chef relished in the dramatization, the hand movements, how Fenton's face demonstrated the bar of which one's expectations ought to be.

"You really do explain each dish spot on, Fenton. I wish you could be at every table," the chef gushed near the end of the shift, after the special had sold out.

"You guys make that part easy, Chef," Fenton told him.

The chef put his hand on Fenton's shoulder and nodded with a proud smile. Fenton nodded and smiled back. He knew he should feel special getting the chef's approval and he did just for the sake of getting clout in front of the other employees, but this wasn't his first rodeo. He knew what he knew from experience, from work, and he knew when to step up and say so. That hadn't happened to him over night. But with the experience, with the credentials, his enthusiasm needed more pushing. At the end of the day, he had to play the game. He had to pay his cellphone bill like everyone else. Or maybe not like everyone else, considering some of the younger coworkers. He went out the back door to join Rell for a cigarette. Fenton didn't really smoke but he didn't mind an excuse for a break, if only to be outside and take a breath, take a smoke, take a moment to recognize he was still on planet Earth and not some Mojoverse.

"You hitting up anything tonight, playboy?" Fenton asked Rell after a long exhale of menthol.

"I'ma swing by my boy Royal's after we clock out and scoop a nug, then go see about shorty at the Blue Nile. We'll be posted up. You looking to get on one tonight?"

"After that last night at the Den, you got a nigga jonesin' for that vibe each and every Wednesday, son. Bet that!" Fenton laughed. Rell started laughing too, loudly, pitching forward, his hand out. Fenton caught the hand and they fell into an embrace, the two of them shaking.

"Not even frontin'. Chick had me twisted," Fenton laughed some more.

"I seent you. Come holler then."

"Word up," Fenton said, the two of them clapping their hands together again in a dap. "I was just peeping last time. Might have to jump up in that circle tonight. Watch how a nigga roll for real, for real."

Fenton had his hand out for another dap but saw Rell freeze up and look past him. Instinctively, Fenton straightened his posture and spun around, a lightning bolt of vulnerability flashing through him. Standing in the door was the chef, his expression also frozen, his mouth open and his eyes reflecting a mild level of shock. It shouldn't have been so transparent but there was no mistaking it. Their eyes met, and Fenton felt a rash of shame prickle up his back. The chef smiled awkwardly, like he'd just walked in on his parents having a private conversation, and he turned around, disappearing back into the restaurant. Fenton turned back to Rell, pursing his lips.

Rell was smirking again but it wasn't the same as before. It wasn't his smug smirk.

"Yup. The boss done seen you now. Sorry, nigga."

The two of them stood out there the rest of their cigarette, neither saying a word.

TIME HEALS

Jude swung open the screen door of his shotgun apartment and let in his friend. When he closed the door, they hugged.

"I brought beer," his buddy Fenton said.

"Yeah. The fridge. C'mon," Jude said.

He opened the case and took out two and brought them to the couch and they sat down. The television was on. ESPN. They stared at it a while. The Cavs were playing the Knicks. Wasn't looking like a good season for either of them. But the Cavs were ahead.

"How's things," Fenton asked.

"Ah not bad. Got a raise at work."

"That's good."

"Thinking about buying a house."

"Oh wow."

They drank more beer. When they smoked cigarettes, they went out on the porch. Fenton didn't really smoke anymore but he went outside anyway.

"I'm dating a girl. It's getting serious," Fenton said.

"Really?"

"Yeah. We talk about shit all the time. Future shit."

"Look at you. I wondered if it would ever happen."

"Yeah well, we'll see."

Jude had some whiskey on the top of his fridge. They got into that, taking shots with their beers.

"When's the last time you talked to Rachel?" Fenton asked.

"Couple weeks ago," Jude said.

"How'd that go?"

Jude shrugged. "Eh."

"You get to see the kids at all?"

"Once a month now."

"I'm sure you miss 'em."

"Something fierce," Jude said.

"They're growing up."

"Bigger every time I see 'em."

Jude's chin dipped and his shoulders started shaking. Fenton frowned and looked around and then back at Jude. He put his hand on Jude's shoulder.

"It'll get better, bud. You'll see."

"I don't know. I just wish I'd never done it. I wish it all the time. I wish I'd seen it coming. It got all so damn built up."

"Now you know, though. Now you know and you won't let it get that bad with the next one. Therapy isn't a bad thing, man. And you cool it, with this stuff." Fenton waved his beer with two fingers. He sighed. "Everyone knows that wasn't you. It was god awful but it wasn't you, Jude."

"But it was. I did that to her. I'm lucky that's all I did. I'm lucky I'm not still in jail. I should be in jail. A man does that to a woman. He deserves to rot."

"People make mistakes, bud. And time heals."

"Time. Time's all I fucking got. I got too much time."

Fenton looked at the television. The Knicks had come back and won. Lebron looked real sad, like he was wondering if he'd made a mistake. Fenton poured them another shot.

FAST NIGHTS AT THE HIGHBALL

It was a beautiful afternoon in Austin, and the city was still a cool place to be, but its days were numbered and anybody who could tell their head from their ass knew it. As far as the weather went, it was the ideal time of the year. You could still go outside and not melt into a puddle in a split second. Not see the quivering mirage deceptively beckoning on the horizon. You could finally be spared a day of questioning why you submit yourself to this, day after day. You could step out of the AC and feel strong and look handsome and that's how I felt. I had ridden my sleek blue Cannondale to Rooster's early and now I was sitting on his couch with his dog Trudy, watching a flick while he was in the shower. I was watching Denzel in *Man on Fire*. It was my favorite Denzel movie. If you asked me, I'd tell you it's because I liked revenge.

Rooster was putting on a shirt when he walked into the living room. He walked in right at my favorite part. Denzel had the gun on the father who had been dealing dirty with the cops and his wife was about to find out.

"You love Denzel," Rooster said.

"This is my favorite part," I said, standing up.

Denzel said, "You move . . . you make one sound . . . and I'll snatch the life right out of your chest, you understand?"

"Whooo!" We both went and high fived. I turned the TV off.

"We meeting Ollie in the park?"

"Yup," I said.

"Let me grab my gift."

Rooster went back to his bedroom and returned with a small box. I picked up my box as well, which was much larger and tied with a bow.

"Damn. Show off," Rooster said. I just grinned.

I was doing well financially. I wasn't being smart with the money, but I was having a lot of fun. No big surprise there. I was actually making the most money I'd ever made in my life, but instead of paying off my student loans or doing anything responsible at all, I was buying new Hawaiian shirts every week, settling entire tabs of strangers at the bar, and booking trips in the middle of the night to places it took eight hours minimum to get to. Still, the weather was indeed beautiful, and I loved my pals, truly, and I'd never ate so well in my life. Honestly, I think I was genuinely surprised to have made it this far. I knew I'd earned it, maybe even deserved it, but now that I was here, you couldn't expect me to act right. Not when I'd had at least three teachers at different points in my life tell me I was surely headed to jail. And I went there. But I just went other places too. Look at me here in Austin. I think I was beginning to at least grasp the idea of new money, and why the old money was always so disdainful. How quickly the rose wilted. I was reckless as hell. But fuck 'em. Rooster, Ollie, and I were all off on the same day. We were fixing to give this town a new coat of paint.

Ollie was sitting on a bench in the park facing the creek. There was a tiny breeze and it lifted her blond hair and it almost looked like a fairy tale until she turned around and we saw her red lipstick and we remembered this was not some sweet damsel but our She-Wolf, one of the deadliest things you could encounter in the wild.

"Hey boys, how we feeling?" she said in her good Southern

drawl. "Bright-eyed and bushy-tailed?" She stood up, her gift lying on the bench, wrapped in newspaper. The funnies.

"I ain't even go out last night," I said.

"Bullshit," Rooster said.

"Well, not all night. Just a quick boy."

"Another Hawaiian shirt, Levy?" Ollie said, hands on her hips.

"New week, new Hawaiian."

"What sense does that make?"

"Yeah," I said.

The three of us stood there, laughing, each now cradling a gift. I handed mine to Rooster. Ollie handed hers to me. Rooster handed his to Ollie. This was a tradition we'd started. We did it every other week, just a funny and sweet way we came up with to start the day we'd all have off together, before we'd commence running around terrorizing the establishments and citizens of the city. I guess we were all kind of doing all right. And all three of us were floating too. None of us knew what we wanted to do, where we wanted to go, who we wanted to be. So we'd gripped onto this thing we could do together, knowing full well it couldn't last forever. But while we were in it, we were all the way in it, and we were loyal and serious about it, and, though I couldn't speak for the other two, I felt it made me better at the things I was already doing. It made me better at my job, made me better at walking into a room, shaped what clothes I wore and what music I listened to and what drink I ordered at a bar. Maybe I knew how to do those things before, but I'd never felt I did it so truly as myself up until those days, when the three of us were out doing whatever we wanted. That's how I felt anyway. Feelings were fleeting, of course. Feelings change. But here we were, grown adults handing each other presents in a park on a beautiful day like we were kids at recess and we all shared the same birthday.

We each opened our presents, wrapping paper falling to the green grass. I got mine open first.

"*Trouble Is My Business* by Raymond Chandler . . . Vintage edition. Goddamn, Ollie. How'd you know I love this guy?"

"You were at work talking about *The Big Sleep* the other night . . . I know you were talking about the movie with Bogart but I looked it up and saw that it was based off this guy's book. I was scared you might already have it, actually."

"I don't have this one. Goddamn. Thank you so much. You really are a sweetheart," I told her.

Ollie and Rooster opened up their presents at the same time. Ollie had a brand new taser in her hand and Rooster held a medieval flail. The real thing. Wooden handle, chain, and a ball hanging on the end of it with protruding spikes. Rooster laughed and gave me a big hug. Ollie looked at the two of us with her mouth open.

"Y'all two really got some problems," she said.

"Hey, Ollie, that's for protection," Rooster said.

"And what the hell is that ungodly thing for?" she asked him.

"To crush his enemies, see them driven before him, and hear the lamentations of their women," I quoted *Conan*. Rooster laughed. "Hand 'em over. We gotta get this day rollin'."

We stuffed all the presents into my backpack. We left the park. We started to move fast. We knew the routine. Food and light afternoon cocktails first. Give our bodies some foundation, the sustenance which would provide the necessary fortitude against all the abuse we were about to inflict on ourselves. I'd already tossed my bike in the bed of Rooster's truck. We piled into the front seat, the three of us together. We rolled down the windows and cranked up the tunes and barreled downtown to La Condesa. Austin had some good happy hours, but this was one of the best if you wanted to go far into the night and not have too much weight on you. We got a bunch of tacos, some guac, elotes, and we each got different types of margaritas with the Tajín rim. The general manager, who was a dear friend of ours, came over with a tray of shots. We took those down and I stood up and started doing my half-ass version of a salsa dance, one hand in the air, and everyone laughed and begged me to sit down, to quit looking so stupid, but we were happy and none of us really minded and, in fact, knew it was vital to the day, to the ride. The dance was essential for what the day stood for and for what we wanted in life. People looked wildly over their shoulders to behold us in alarm but because everyone in their sight and within our company was smiling and laughing and beautiful, it was accepted and regarded in awe, like who were these people? What made them special? What could I do to gain such hospitality? But if you had to wonder, you'd probably end up wondering the rest of your life.

We left that place, sauced, but nowhere near our intended destinations. I gave the general manager a big kiss on the way out and we stumbled out the door and down the sidewalk in broad daylight like a trio of old-world traveling bards freshly home from years out on the azure sea. It was a Tuesday afternoon for God's sake. People in business attire passed us on the street questioning our entire resume of choices in life. It wasn't as if we didn't participate in these petty judgments as well. We just reserved it for when we were at work, serving the privileged pompous ding-dongs of the world. Reserve your loathing, citizen, we were off the clock.

It was still an hour or so before the sun would start to head down. We parked in the lot in front of Highball. I took my bike out the bed of the truck to lock up to the rack in front of the venue.

I knew this place could end up being where the road split for the party. I wasn't planning on riding the bike home because that would be suicide if I was too far gone, but if I left it in Rooster's truck, I knew I'd forget it all together. Leaving it here overnight wasn't a huge risk. Forgetting it in Rooster's truck was just plain dumb, which I could be at least twice a week. I had my backpack slung over my shoulder and we all walked into the place.

"We want the Van Halen room," I said at the counter, slamming my fist down for emphasis.

I did this every time. If we ever had someone new in our posse, they would get scared by my aggression. But the employees knew us well, knew my routine well. No one was new here. The girl rolled her eyes, took my bank card for the deposit, and handed us some menus.

"Hand over your backpack," the girl said, monotone.

I smiled and did so. Her arm sagged from the weight.

"The hell is in here?" she asked, face scrunched up.

"Do not open that bag or I'll sue your ass. Listen, we already know what we want. A bucket of High Life. A round of shots. Whiskey. Go ahead and add some cheese fries."

"You know full well you wait until your server comes into the room to give them your order, jag-off," the girl told me.

"Please don't hate me," I plead.

"Then don't act like a jerk, Levy."

"Yeah. Don't act like a jerk, Lev," Ollie echoed, grinning and digging a finger into my cheek. Rooster put his arm around my shoulder. The girl led us to our room with a sassy snap to her hip. She unlocked the door and held out her hand to usher us inside, the large television on the wall glowing in the dark like the window to a spaceship, stars glistening into the infinite darkness.

I picked up the remote control like I was in my own living

room and flipped it in the air. I caught it and I was surprised but I looked at Rooster and Ollie anyway, like a kid who'd just learned how to ride his bike without training wheels, and we all started laughing again.

We didn't have our backpack full of weapons and relics but as I was selecting the first song of the day, Ollie pulled out a small bag of cocaine and emptied enough to start carving out three lines. I chose Rod Stewart's "You Wear It Well." Rooster clapped me on the back then dipped down for the first snort of the night.

Within the span of a few songs, the three of us had that room raging like a Mötley Crüe video. Our server was a lanky, goofy white kid with hair that fell over his eyes. I'd slap his ass any time I got the opportunity, but never if he was holding a full tray. I was what you called a part-time gentleman. He didn't partake in our party goods, though we offered. Nevertheless, every other round of shots, he'd accept the invitation and clink a glass with us. He especially liked Ollie's Reba McEntire covers.

We'd been in there a couple hours, though in reality we had no concept of time within that place, and maybe spending hours in a karaoke room with just three people might seem peculiar to another person, but for the three of us, we simply didn't need anything else. Or if we did, we had a button we could press, and a sweet young man with a high level of tolerance for abuse would appear, happy to bring us anything we requested, as long as it was on the menu. I was standing on the couch singing "In Dreams" by good old Roy Orbison, leaning back against the white shag carpet wall, swaying, Ollie and Rooster opposite the room, seated and watching me dreamily, when the television exploded with an incredibly loud boom and a shower of sparks and debris. The three of us all reeled back, screaming like the world was ending, this secret world we'd made for ourselves.

I leapt down to the floor. I don't know where the hell the mic had gone, which worried me briefly because there was a hefty deposit you lost if you damaged anything in the room, which I'd done once before and swore I never would again. Without the glow of the television, the room was completely dark now.

"Are you guys OK?" I asked meekly.

"Did the TV just blow up?" Ollie asked.

"What did you do, Levy?" Rooster asked.

"Oh, shut up," I whispered.

I crept on all fours to where I thought the door was and pulled it open. The light from the hallway flooded in. I peeked my head outside. There was no one there. I stood up and turned on the light to the room. Rooster and Ollie were on the floor too and they'd kicked the table and caused beer bottles to fall over. Only a couple were broken. The fucking fries were all over the place.

In seconds, our server and the girl from the front desk showed up in our room. By then we were all standing, hands on our hips, surveying the destruction of the room. Luckily, I'd done as good a job as I could of hiding the narcotic usage. Still, the two employees regarded us in horror.

"Levy," the girl from the front desk whispered, "What did you do?"

That was when we all heard a scream. A woman's scream. And from the hole in the wall where the television had only minutes ago hung, we could understand the scream was coming from the room on the other side of us. The Ruby Room.

They called it the Ruby Room because the walls and the couches inside were all furnished with a plush red sparkling leather. The police showed up and in heavy numbers, quickly securing the room, building, and otherwise. A pair of ambulances followed. It had been a Latino couple in the Ruby Room. Their first time together at the Highball. The man, trying to shield his lady the best he could, had taken whatever of the shotgun blast that hadn't hit the wall and burst the television in the next room. He was dead, but he hadn't died quickly. He'd taken his last breath cradled in her arms. She was a little scraped up, but her injuries were not serious. They would still take her in to the hospital.

She hysterically told the cops she suspected it was her crazy ex-boyfriend, but she couldn't be sure. The room had been dark after all, and when the door had opened mid song, all she could really see was his silhouette. The man had lifted the rifle and her boyfriend had then blocked her vision, saving her life, sacrificing his own. True fucking love. But she told the cops she could recognize his figure, and that they themselves used to come here.

"He would never sing but he would sit there and watch me," she told the cops from her gurney, her dark hair splayed back and a mess. Her eyes were big and it was if she couldn't see what was in front of her. Like she was trying to see what was behind who was in front of her. "He could watch me for as many songs as I wanted to sing and never complain. Like, he was mesmerized. He'd never say it like that though. He don't know big words like that. He wasn't very bright." She was talking like she'd woken up from a dream, like none of this had really happened. When she realized once again that it had, that's when the nightmares would come.

They wheeled her off to the other ambulance and questioned us next. We all three were nervous as hell. Rooster and Ollie were nervous because of the drugs. I was nervous because of the drugs but also, I was just nervous. You know. Because, cops.

"What were y'all doing when this occurred?" an officer asked us.

"Singing," I told him.

"Who was singing?"

"I was."

"What were you singing?"

"Roy Orbison."

He lifted an eyebrow. "You being funny?"

"No, sir."

I had both hands already behind my back, but I was trying to signal as discreetly yet as frantically as I could. See, I knew where this cop wanted to go. I don't know if I just had that look that made a cop's dick get hard but this wasn't my first rodeo, nor would it be the last. No choice but to accept that reality, and also, truth was: I did break the law. Regularly. But so did most of my white friends. Only difference was, I wasn't white. I still had the small baggie of coke in my back pocket. So I'd pulled it out and was waving it to Ollie so that she'd snatch it up before the predictable went down.

"And so none of you saw anybody in the hall?"

"No, sir."

"Did you look?"

"I did," I admitted.

"Did you ever look in the other room?"

"I did not, sir."

"Looks like you all were having a pretty good time in here," the officer said, surveying the room.

"We were, sir."

"What's up with the tattoos? You a convict?"

"No, sir. I'm a bartender," I answered.

"What the hell kind of question is that?" Rooster demanded, speaking for the first time. It made me smile, but I quickly did my best to suppress that.

"You need to calm down. It's just a question," the officer told him.

"Yeah, but what *kind* of question is it? What's that gotta do with someone being shot in the other room? Why are you questioning us like we're suspects or guilty of anything? We had nothing to do with what happened over there and we could've been hurt and you're asking my friend if he's a convict?"

"I told you to calm down, sir. I'm just doing my job," the officer said, one hand up to Rooster, the national gesture of the cop who was in control, a clear message to relay that you dare not raise your voice a decibel above theirs. The other hand went to his belt like he was Batman or some shit.

As the two of them squared off, Ollie inched up behind me and picked the baggie from my offering hand. She slipped it into her jacket pocket and took a tiny step back.

"It's OK, Roose," I said, quietly relieved.

"It's not OK," he said back to me. He was shaking from anger. God bless him.

"It's my job to figure out what happened."

"Well, we told you what happened. Can we go now? We don't have anything else to say to you."

"We're gonna need you to stick around a little bit longer. We're gonna have to search you."

"Oh, to hell with that. You're not searching us and none of us are saying a damn thing else."

I could see the officer boiling up. He hadn't expected Rooster's fury and he really wanted to do something about it. An officer showed up behind him and said something under his breath, then looked at the three of us. The questioning officer bit his lip, his ideas of what he wanted to do with us projecting out of his eyes like a Confederate-owned drive-in theater.

"Y'all should leave immediately. I don't want to see any of y'all driving either."

The two officers left. I let out a deep breath of air and started laughing right after. Ollie put her hand to her forehead.

"Fucking pig," Rooster said.

"It's OK, Roose," I repeated.

"No, man. That's ridiculous. I know you probably deal with that all the time but it's ridiculous. Power tripping fucktard."

"Let's get the hell out of here. Playtime is over."

"Is it?" Ollie said, flashing the baggie from her pocket. We all three started grinning. I realized I had become as sober as a nun in all the excitement. It made me a little sad, but I felt more sad for the dead boyfriend. Maybe one day she'll sing a song for you, old boy.

"Let's get the hell out of here. My place. We can hit the park next door," I said.

We left the room and went up to the front counter. The girl was there. She had two pink hair clips in her dark hair. I hadn't noticed before. She handed over my backpack. I hitched it over my shoulder.

"You guys don't have to pay anything tonight. I asked the manager and he said it was cool. You could've been hurt. Somebody died for Christ's sake."

"Damn. That's really considerate of y'all. This shit is crazy. Are you OK?" I asked her.

"I don't know yet," she said.

"Hey, listen. We really appreciate you guys. Here, this is for you and Shaggy." I put two hundred-dollar bills on the counter and slid it over.

"You're really sweet, Levy," she tilted her head.

"Don't tell nobody."

We got out of there. It was night outside. Still warm. The parking lot was lit up with cop cars and not in the fun way.

I started unlocking my bike. "I'm gonna ride to my place.

Probably smart to follow that jackass's advice and leave the truck here, bub. Cab over?"

"We're on it. You safe to ride?" Rooster asked me.

"I'm safe to ride. Here, do me a favor. Carry this bag for me," I removed it from my back and handed it over to him. "Remember the address?"

Just as Rooster was saying it out loud, the second cop who had come in to retrieve the first from the Van Halen room came out the doors , walking towards us. We stopped talking to look at him.

"I want to apologize for my coworker," he started. "He takes the job very seriously." Ollie scoffed. He offered a card to her anyway. "In case anything comes up, you recall anything, anything that can help us. We'd really appreciate it. I'm sorry your night got ruined. This was awful stuff."

He walked back inside.

"He seemed nice," Ollie said, checking out his card.

"Bullshit," I spit on the asphalt. "Being polite once when your people aren't around doesn't make up for your whole outfit being a pack of sons of bitches. Gimme that."

Ollie handed me the card. I ripped it in four pieces and flicked it into the street. The night was swirling red and blue, all mixed up with the fluorescent parking lights, higher up. The moon should've been somewhere up there, behind the clouds that were moving faster than they ought to. I guess the moon was somewhere else. Not here.

"Be safe, Levy," Ollie called out to me once I was on the bike. I gave a curt wave. I wanted to get the hell out of there. I'd been able to keep my composure around the cops, but the truth was I always felt an incredible rage in the aftermath. Because maintaining that control was so necessary, but it always came with a cost. And now, alone again, I needed to release the pent-up energy. Besides the one dip that went underneath the bridge, the shot down Lamar Boulevard was almost all downhill. I pedaled fast, bombing down the street as fast as I could, no helmet. The wind streaked over me. I gripped the handlebars like it was the steering wheel of a fighter jet.

Once I rose up from the one dip on the route, pedaling hard, I could hear an engine behind me, coming up fast. There was a red light ahead. I thought for a second it might be the cab Rooster and Ollie were in. But cabbies don't drive like that unless you're late for the airport.

Instead of stopping at the light, I barreled right through. I didn't check to see if there was crossing traffic. I was banking on the time of night to keep the street empty and I won my bet. I went through the light without losing my life and once I got to the other side, I chanced a look back. It was a faded-looking gray Neon, a man who barely fit in the car behind the wheel. He looked like he'd played linebacker once upon a time. I couldn't see his face.

I was going downhill once more, but I started pedaling hard anyway. It didn't feel right. On occasion, I was known to be paranoid but any smart black dude living in America ought to be if he wanted to make it. The trick was to know when to stay cool and when to lose your shit, and right now, alone in the night, this was when you had to be the coolest. I looked back. The Neon was coming on. I had a few more streets up. One more light to give the Neon the stall, if the driver decided he wanted to obey the law, that is. I could hear the engine again, revving.

I made it to the light and once again the Neon slowed. I was at the final hill's descent. My apartment was at the bottom, along with the park. The street was pitch black here. I wasn't even halfway down the street before there were lights beaming from behind me, lighting me up. My shirt was soaked from sweat. I bombed down the hill. To the left was my apartment. I didn't stop. I went straight for the park. There was a curb, but I didn't slow down for that either. I stood up on the pedals and right when the front tire hit the cement, I let the momentum catapult me forward. I felt the night air caress me. I pulled myself into a ball, legs tucking underneath me, hands outstretched. I rolled forward into soft grass I couldn't see but knew was there. The impact, for me, was minimal. I heard my bike crunch and, just after that, the Neon screech behind me. I rolled neatly to my feet and started running into the darkness of the park, where there was no light, just the dark giants of the forest.

Biking everywhere in Austin had kept me in good shape, and I knew where I was going. I thought I did anyway. I looked behind me. The Neon was at the edge of the park. The engine was no longer on, and neither were the headlights. I kept running. Up ahead was a wooden bridge. A shallow stream was underneath it. I couldn't even hear it. The water must've been that low.

I reached the bridge and skidded down the side, down gravel that hissed beneath my black Vans. I crept under the wooden slats. I could feel the water, the slime of the rocks. The stream was barely moving. I could feel webs hanging from the bridge sticking to my head. My heartbeat was punching my chest plate. I tried holding my breath as a way to slow my gasps for air.

For a while, I didn't hear anything besides the shrieks of my own fear. I wondered if whoever was chasing me had given up. I wondered who in the hell it could even be. I hadn't really made any enemies in Austin yet. Or maybe I had. Maybe I didn't remember. Maybe it was someone from Richmond. They'd recognized me on the street and decided this was the perfect time.

From underneath the little bridge, I could see a light darting overhead. I took a deep breath and quit breathing after that. I could begin to hear the footsteps now. Soft. Contemplative. Then the first step on the wooden slats of the bridge just above my head. The owner of the foostep lingered there. I imagined the owner, guessing in the dark, wondering where this path would lead him to. I prayed he would keep going, because I knew how far on the trail went, but my prayer would not be answered. The body left the bridge and returned to the earth. I laid there, in the water and the rocks and the spiderwebs, watching the flashlight descend, inevitably to where I lay to finally shine upon me. I could only see thick brown fingers, holding the light.

"Why you hiding?" a deep voice asked me.

I didn't say anything. I thought if I did, I'd pop like a firecracker.

"When people run," the shroud said, "it's 'cause they don't wanna be caught. They don't wanna be caught 'cause they're afraid. They got something to hide. So . . . why you hiding?"

The shroud was breathing hard and since I had nowhere to go, I started breathing again too.

"What do you want from me?" I asked him raggedly.

"Depends. What did you see back there? When you were singing your songs?"

I swallowed thickly, like there were paper towels in my throat. My mind was going in all different directions.

"I didn't see anything. I didn't know them, I didn't see nothing, and I didn't tell the cops nothing."

We were quiet. The shroud kept the light right on my face. I saw nothing. Just those fingers.

"Maybe. I saw you rip up the card. Out front. So maybe you're right."

Quiet again. The forest was absolute silence. Just the two of them breathing, and finally, even that was calming. A terrible and scary calm.

"Then again," the shroud said, and now I could see the barrel of a shotgun lift into the range of the flashlight. "There ain't no one who would know out here anyway. Better to be safe, huh? Bad luck. You ain't a bad singer."

I stared at the light, the metal of the rifle.

"Fuck you," I said.

The shroud started chuckling. Holding the flashlight at the same time, that hand with the big fingers pulled back on the shotgun.

A cloud passed us, the final one, and walking in the room like the girl of your dreams, was the moon, full and serene. A buzz clicked in the air and I heard the shroud gurgle and suddenly the flashlight and the gun fell to the rocks with a clatter. A heavy thud followed that.

I crawled out from under the bridge, soaked. The light from a cellphone illuminated me in blue.

"Lev!"

I bent down and picked up the flashlight. Lying at my feet was the shaking body of a very thick fellow, baseball cap worn backwards. Sticking out of him were two little prongs with wires attached to them, and the wires traced back to a taser held by none other than my dear sweet Ollie.

Rooster skidded down the gravel until he stood next to me. He scooped up the shotgun, then looked at me, his face pale.

"Dude! Are you OK?"

I was staring at him with my mouth open. But then I started grinning.

"We found your bike at the edge of the park. The front tire's so bent it looks like a boomerang. Who the fuck is this guy?"

"Ollie," I said, and the irony wasn't lost on me when I said it, "Call 911."

The big guy began to stir as the charge of the taser wore off. He groaned. I was holding the flashlight on him, but now that we were no longer under the bridge and the moon was once again with us, we were able to have a general view of where we all were positioned. The big guy sat up.

Rooster pointed the shotgun at him. "You back with us, huh? Listen up, hoss. The cops are on the way. We're all gonna sit right here. You move . . . you make one sound . . . and I'll snatch the life right out of your chest, you understand?"

Rooster couldn't see me, but I was grinning like hell. I put a hand on his shoulder.

The cops got there fast, once again. Must've been a slow night in Austin. Kids must've been in school. The bastards drove right into the grass, tearing the green all up. They had the park lit up like it was a circus. By then, they'd already seen the videotape from the Highball and were able to confirm the big guy matched the figure who had run in and out of the venue. They led him off in cuffs. They confiscated the shotgun. Once again, we were being questioned.

"So you didn't know this guy?" the officer, the same damn officer was asking me.

"We didn't, sir."

"But he followed you down here. To your place."

"Well, my place is just before the park. I don't live under a bridge, sir. But yes," I said.

"I know you don't live under a damn bridge, boy."

"Just making sure," I said, holding my hand up, trying to keep some of his flashlight off my face.

"Is this your backpack?"

"Yes, sir."

"This is *your* backpack?"

"Yes it is, sir."

"Can you tell me what the hell this thing is?"

He pulled out the flail I'd bought for Rooster.

"It's a present for my friend here, sir."

Rooster and Ollie stood next to me, both of them grinning like moonlit demons.

HOW MANY OF US

Fenton's phone was buzzing. The screen said "Dad." When Fenton answered, his dad went, "My number one son!"

"Hey, Dad," Fenton said, keeping his tone monotone even though he was smiling. "How are you?"

"I'm good! I'm good. How are you?"

"Yeah, I'm hanging in there."

"Staying out of trouble?"

"Well, you know me . . ."

"Yeah, I know you," he said, laughing. It made Fenton smile even wider, whether he wanted to or not. Somewhere along the way, Fenton's dad had figured out who his son was. And upon the discovery, he was still all right with it. His dad still liked him. He liked how his son had turned out, even if he wasn't rich or had a nice car or a nice house or straight teeth. It was a relief, knowing that, knowing his love was for real. Fenton understood not every kid got that from their parents. Not when they're young, not when they're grown, maybe just never. And on his end, Fenton loved his dad very much. And he mostly liked him a lot too. But it was harder for him to like his father all the way. He was his son, after all. Fenton realized his father was human, and thus fallible, but Fenton was a still judgy bastard. He could say he got it from his mother, but it was too late for that anymore. The excuses. This was who he was now. Fenton accepted his character solemnly and without reservation.

"How you doing with the sugar and all, Pop?" he asked.

"Man, I'm doing way better. Way better. Doc says I'm at an all-time low."

"Really?"

"Yeah, really!"

"How many Cokes you drinking a day?"

"I'm hardly drinking any!"

"How many, Dad?" Fenton pressed him.

"Shoot, I barely drink one. One or two."

"Dad!"

"No, it's usually just one. You know that's good for me. You know how it was. Shoot, weekends I might go without one at all. So just one or two a day. That's it. Not the Big Gulps either. I never do the Big Gulps anymore. Made your Mom a promise on that one. Just the cans now. Helps me measure it better. So about one or two a day. I bet one day soon I won't be drinking any at all. Watch."

Fenton sighed heavily, looking out the windshield of his car. "OK, Dad. I know you can do it. I believe in you. I'm proud of you. You got this."

"Yeah, I got this. Don't worry about me, boy."

"I do worry about you though, Dad. Your heart can't take the sugar anymore."

"Don't worry, son. I promise. I got this. I promise."

Fenton got off the phone with his dad a little while later, after sharing some safe details of his own life. Things that would make his dad feel good about getting off the phone with him. Fenton was on his way to work. They kept it short and sweet, like everyone in their family did. It was just easier that way. No one had to worry. No one had to feel guilty. Their own secret troubles were enough, no one really wanted to carry any more.

Fenton stopped off at a corner café to get some coffee before the shift. He kept his sunglasses on when he got inside, and didn't look around for anyone that he knew. He ordered a mocha latte. Inevitably, someone said his name.

"Fenton."

He sighed and looked up and saw it was Pearson. Pearson was a little taller than Fenton was and he wore glasses, the regular kind, and he was handsome in a normal way, but not exactly for this time or this city. They were in New Orleans. He was a white guy that came from money who wanted to be a bartender when his family had probably expected him to be a professor or a dentist or something like that. Pearson liked being a bartender, but thought he still owned the rights to the condescending attitude that an academic elite might bestow upon themself. Fenton didn't mind Pearson too much, but could only take their interactions in doses.

"Got work tonight?" Pearson asked.

"Yup."

"Yeah, me too. Right up the block."

"Yeah."

"You usually get off around midnight this time of the week, right?"

"That's right."

"I get off around that time. Stop by for a drink, your first one will be on me."

"Yeah, OK, Pearson."

"Mocha latte?" a lady behind the counter called out.

"I'll see you, Pearson."

"OK, Fin."

Fenton got his latte and got out of there. He loved New Orleans, but New Orleans was a small city and this neighborhood was even smaller. I have to start getting my coffee somewhere else, he told himself once again. But Pearson's not so bad, really. Not really.

When Fenton got to work, Edson was sitting outside of the bar on a weatherworn and rickety stool, puffing on a Winston cigarette. Edson was only a couple years older than Fenton, but he looked like he was at least twenty years older. He had nice hair, no gray yet, still bright somehow, and he wore it in a long ponytail, like a memento, like a scarf a beautiful woman might have worn wrapped around her slender neck. It was in his face though. His face looked like it could have been beaten out of the side of a mountain. Deep creases, rough, worn, like it had been there for forever, looking out into world, and had seen more than Fenton could possibly fathom.

Edson liked to refer to himself as "white trash." He laughed when he said it, and therefore so would Fenton. That was all on him. Kinda how a woman will tell you she's a crazy bitch and you know never to call her one yourself, yet you believe her fully. Fenton would laugh with Edson, knowing it to be true, and he appreciated that Edson didn't have any desire to hide it. That he was willing to be like: Hey, this is who I am. No bullshit.

Edson was a cook at the bar, which didn't say a lot if it was your only gig. But then, Fenton had been working at the bar for a couple years now. That surprised him too. Just a couple shifts a week between another couple restaurants, like some kind of mercenary, but way less exciting. Well, sometimes. Sometimes it could get pretty damn exciting. But mostly he liked working at a place like this to mix it up from the fancier spots he worked the other nights. Fenton liked the duality. He enjoyed living in multiple worlds.

Back in the early days, the first days, sitting outside smoking cigarettes, he'd asked the cook: "Where you from, Edson?"

"Indiana," he told Fenton.

"Dang. I've never met anyone from up there. What do you do in Indiana?"

Edson took a long drag and flicked his Winston out into the street. "You go to jail in Indiana."

Fenton laughed his ass off to that. He thought it sounded cool. Edson smiled, but he didn't laugh. That's how Fenton knew he meant it.

That day, that shift, he came up to Edson and they shook hands and Fenton said, "How's it looking in there?"

"Looking good for me," he said, squinting at me. "Just waiting on my paycheck. I got the next two days off."

"Nice. What you gonna do?"

"Fixing to ride the lightning, Fin."

"Ha. All right. Just make sure you don't crash like thunder."

Edson stuck his hand out to him and Fenton took it. "My dude," he said. Fenton went on inside the bar.

There were some people at the bar, but it wasn't anything crazy. Fresh off of work, they typically only stuck around for one or two drinks. Richelle was stirring a cocktail and shaking a tin behind the bar and winked at Fenton as he entered. He smiled, thinking, what a pro.

"There he is," one of the regulars announced Fenton's arrival.

He put his jacket in the back and got behind the bar. He put a dish rag in one of his belt loops and stretched.

"How you feeling?" Richelle asked.

"Not bad," he told her.

"Might get busy tonight," she said.

"Kick the tires and light the fires, babe."

The early regulars came and went and then the real crowd rolled in, and they were seemingly relentless for a little while, giddy from getting off work, eager for that taste they'd had on their fading minds that last crawling hour, and Fenton and Richelle felt the force of them. There was no time to talk or joke or check their phones, but the two of them worked well together and Fenton could anticipate her needs and where her body would move next and they weathered the storm. Finally, when it eased up and he knew they would be OK, Fenton said to her, "I'm gonna step outside for a quick one," and she smiled faintly and nodded. He went out through the kitchen, out onto the side of the bar. There were some people talking out there, so he walked the opposite direction. He tried his best not to interact too much with the guests at this bar. He sort of didn't have to. It wasn't a place any schmoozing was necessary. The money was there. He was sure his boss probably wished he were a little nicer, but Fenton's mentality was you needed at least one guy like him on every team. Richelle was a sweetie. Everyone loved her. That took the pressure off Fenton. Have a nice time with Richelle but understand you won't be pulling any shit on this shift, not while he around. There was another guy at the bar who was an actual asshole, but the main difference between he and Fenton was the guy tried to act like he wasn't one. The guy just couldn't help himself really. Fenton tried his best not to ever work a shift with the man. It usually worked out.

The night came and went. It was pleasant as always working with Richelle, playing good music, sharing a drink here and there. The clientele eased on out and he let her leave first. He was only an hour or so after her. He took his time shutting the place down, playing some slow weird metal he liked to listen to when he had the place to himself with the lights down low. The place had a decent sound system even if the roof was caving in.

Fenton put the till back in the office and, as always, made to sure lock everything up properly. He took one more shot of

Montenegro for the road, put in the code for the security system, locked up the doors, and was home free.

He wasn't hungry and he wasn't tired but he knew it'd be smart to be close to home if he was gonna get a night cap or two, and he knew he was gonna get a night cap or two. He wasn't very enthusiastic about it but he decided to take Pearson up on that drink.

He pulled up to the bar and Pearson was outside the place smoking. He raised a hand. Fenton got out of the car and walked up. They shook hands.

"How was the shift?" Pearson asked him.

"Nothing bad. You?"

"Same. Wanna drink?"

"Yup."

They went inside. The music was loud. The door guy nodded to Fenton and he nodded back. They got up to the bar and Pearson held up two fingers. The bartender put two bottles of High Life on the counter paired with two shots of tequila.

"No whiskey?" Fenton asked.

"I'm trying to get off the stuff."

"Were you a bad boy?"

"Just trying to be better. I'm married now."

"I heard. Congratulations."

"Thanks. I'm not ever gonna be a saint but I figure why not try to clean up my act any kind of fraction? Little here, little there."

"I think that's admirable, Pearson."

"I do too," he said, proud of himself. They held up the shots and took them down. It was nice. They took some stools at a high table next to the mirrored wall and in a corner a television was playing *Barberella*. Fenton realized he'd never watched this movie any other time where it wasn't muted or playing outside of some bar. Multiple cities. It was funny to him.

The two of them talked about the Saints and movies and then Pearson went up to the bar for another round of the same. Fenton thought it would end there but it didn't. In truth, nothing had to end in New Orleans if you didn't want it to. That was the magic. And the danger. So, it kept going. A handful of people showed up they mutually knew. Fenton ended up going to the counter a few times himself, plus people brought over whatever. Fenton was laughing his ass off and taking drags off of people's cigarettes just so he could have some kind of connection to them, more of a connection, something more in this world to hold them here, anchor all of them, because time was passing assuredly but they were no longer a part of any of that, they were in this bar where there was no sun or moon or stars, no past or future, just the present, just the now, and all any of them wanted was more. Fenton looked at himself in the mirror, and was happy to see himself staring back.

He stood up and said, "Pearson. I gotta go, man."

"OK," he said.

"You gonna be OK?"

"Yup," he said, smiling, his eyes barely open, but his eyes very bright, nevertheless.

Fenton put his hand on Pearson's shoulder a moment, then walked to the door, walked back to the bar, paid his tab, and finally left that black hole place. The sun wasn't up yet, but he could see the edge of the night running, and he hurried home so he wouldn't have to be ashamed to see his shadow.

Later that morning, Fenton jerked up, naked in bed, to see his phone buzzing. It was his boss from the bar he'd worked at the night before. If his boss was calling this early, Fenton quickly deduced, it had to do with something from last night. And it wouldn't be good.

"I've called you a million times now," his boss said.

"What happened?"

"You closed right?"

"Right."

"We had a burglary."

"Do I need to come in?"

"Fuck yeah, you gotta come in."

"Gimme twenty."

"You got fifteen."

Fenton got up and put last night's clothes on. He went into the bathroom and splashed some water on his face, gurgled some mouth wash. He got his keys, his wallet, and his sunglasses and left. He was there in fifteen.

"What happened? I swear to God, I locked everything up right," Fenton said, walking into the bar. It wasn't lost on him how different the place looked like in the daytime, an almost spectral light flooding into the only two windows, onto the floor and barstools and the countertop. It almost reminded him of a cathedral in a way.

"Don't worry. We got him on video," the guy who was in charge of the kitchen said.

"Got who?" Fenton said, massaging his temples.

"Edson."

"The fuck do you mean, Edson?"

He wasn't lying. The blue video showed the center of the bar. Everything was still, the place was empty. Suddenly, Edson fell from the roof, crashing onto the pool table like a meteor. He laid there for a while, then pulled himself together and got up. He went up the door to the office and started working on the lock. It didn't take him long. He disappeared inside there but when he returned, he had the safe, the size of a microwave. He left through the back door of the bar and that was the last of it. It was Edson all right.

"Holy shit," Fenton said. "He came in through the vent on the roof?"

"Looks like it."

"Did y'all call the police?"

"I wanted to," the boss said.

"Why don't you?"

"We know where he lives," the guy who was in charge of the kitchen said. He wanted to be called chef, but he wasn't one, so Fenton never did.

"So what, you're gonna go over to his place?"

"We all are," the boss said. "We need you on this, Fenton."

"Shiiiiiit," Fenton said, grinning. Then he thought about it. He thought about Edson and himself and this world, all of it. He thought hard about it. Not long, but hard. So that finally, he shrugged. "Fuck it. Let's go."

The boss was driving. Fenton sat shotgun, his sunglasses still on, his mind still a little hazy but beginning to sharpen. "What if he's not there?"

"Where else he's got to go?" the cook asked from the backseat.

"Indiana," Fenton said.

"Indiana?"

"Never mind."

They showed up to the place, supposedly. It was in that small stretch of Mid-City that was more brown than black or white, where the sidewalks were particularly beat-up and broken from neglect and old tree roots. No restaurants or coffee shops but plenty of plastic-cap liquor stores. There was litter everywhere, and ruined vehicles that should've been towed years ago, wheels missing and more rust than paint on them.

"How do you know Edson lives here?" Fenton asked.

"I gave him a ride home from work one night."

"Are we all going to the door?" Fenton asked.

"Yes," the boss said. Fenton looked over at him and started laughing, even though he was a little scared too.

The three of them got out of the car. There were a couple of Hispanic fellows sitting in plastic lawn chairs against a building, not even bothering to hide their tall boys in paper bags. They wore mustaches and their mouths hung open, one of them missing a noticeable number of teeth. Fenton nodded to them. They didn't nod back. The trio walked past.

"He's right up here," the cook said, pointing at the door, looking at Fenton. Fenton looked at his boss. The man was staring at the door. Fenton smiled and shook his head. He walked up the stoop. He knocked three times. The three of them stood there, waiting.

No one answered. Fenton looked at the other two, but they didn't say a word. He balled his hand into a fist and hit the door four times, hard. He leaned in and listened to something moving around in there. They waited some more, Fenton placing himself just on the side of the door frame, out of the way in case anything came flying out. The door had eight glass panes, but they were covered by a thin sheet. Someone there pulled the sheet aside just so. Then the door opened, but only a couple inches, a chain holding it in place.

Fenton half expected a gun to point out at him. Instead, a woman's voice that sounded like a running garbage disposal asked him, "What is it?"

"Edson here?"

"Who're you?"

"I'm his buddy from work. Fenton."

"He's off today."

"Yup. I'm just here to see him."

All he could see was a single hazel eye with some faded make up and creases on the corner. Some dyed orange hair. The door closed. Fenton looked back at the other two. His boss patted the side of his hips. His keys in his pocket.

They stood there for a few minutes. Finally, the door opened wide. It was Edson, wearing some long mesh shorts, a T-shirt that read, "Came in looking for a blonde, got stuck with a Buttface," the sleeves cut off, and a look on his face like he'd just gotten off a rollercoaster that had lasted a month.

"Nice shirt, Edson," Fenton said.

"Fellas?" Edson croaked, genuinely bewildered to see them.

"Edson . . . what the hell?" the cook asked. Fenton thought he was the most angry because he'd hired Edson. He'd vouched for Edson. Fenton liked Edson, but you don't vouch for tweakers. You can't. It doesn't matter if they're nice one day. You don't do it. Because things like this happened. The cook had finally learned that. But now it was *his* ass.

"We got it on video, Edson," the boss said.

"Got what on video?" Edson asked. Fenton was looking him dead in the face. He knew some good liars, and he couldn't get a fix on Edson to save his life. But it wasn't his life. So Fenton just stood there, his arms crossed, his expression maybe like that of a curious child. Fenton knew he was expected to be some kind of tough guy for this role, but he'd quickly come to understand that no one had any real handle on how to navigate the situation they'd all found themselves in.

They had Edson come back to the bar and the four of them watched the video together. No one said a goddamn thing. Fenton felt embarrassed. He knew what was about to happen and this man was about to come face to face with himself. He wasn't going to like what he saw.

"Holy shit," Edson said, when he watched himself burst through the roof.

When the video ended, they all shared that space in silence, contemplating their relationships and the law and where they would all intersect.

Finally, Edson said, "I don't think I can do anything but be honest with y'all right now. You've always been fair to me. I don't remember a damn thing, but that's me, clear as day. I went on a bender and I guess I didn't want it to end. The result was the humiliation of having to endure that video and of course the betrayal I've committed against y'all. I'm fully ashamed of myself. If the next stop is the clink, I won't utter a word of dispute. Y'all done nothing but right by me. I don't even need to stop back home. Yvette will be long gone anyway."

"That your girlfriend?" Fenton asked.

"Nah, she's just a bird."

"Here's the thing, Edson," their boss started. "We could head to the station right now and just let the courts handle it. Have them lock you up and we see you on whatever date they designate. The video says it all. That wouldn't give me any joy, believe it or not, Edson. You been with us a while. And I'm really just at a loss for what step next to take. Despite all this, we don't want bad things for you, Edson."

Fenton was surprised to hear his boss say it, but he stayed quiet, waiting for the other boot to drop.

"But then what? You go to jail, a place you've already been, and we just get nothing? We lose in every scenario here. Edson, what did you do with the money?"

"I don't even remember being in this place past picking up my paycheck. I remember ol' girl coming over with a bag of goodies and it all just seemed to take off from there. If I had to guess,

I burned through the paycheck money and had to find more. I don't remember coming back. I don't remember any further transactions. If I have it . . ."

"If you have it?" the boss said.

"If there's any money left, of course, I'll fork it over. And for whatever's not there . . . I'll pay it back. I swear. It might take me a while, but I swear on my mother's grave, I will. I'm so damn sorry, y'all. You took a chance on me and I let you down. I don't got an excuse. I'm just a rotten scoundrel."

They all stood there, nobody saying nothing, arms crossed and with troubled expressions.

"We gotta go back to my place," Edson said.

The boss, the cook, and Fenton all looked at each other then. Fenton shrugged and smiled, scratching his head.

"I'm off tonight," he said. "I think my part in this is over."

"Fenton . . ." the cook started.

"You guys got this. Or you can get the cops involved. Either way, this is out of my pay grade. I'll see y'all next week. And Edson . . . best of luck, man."

Fenton was driving home thinking, "Poor Edson." That was the destiny of that man. He couldn't save himself. But couldn't he? Weren't they all afforded redemption? Lord knows it was Fenton's favorite kind of story. But he truly believed for some it would be forever out of their grasp, and even further, some he would never have a desire to grant it to. Maybe that was merciless of him, but he had to believe it. Fenton liked Edson, and he liked his doting father too. But some motherfuckers just can't get out of their own way. Would that be my fate as well? Fenton thought They all had their demons. His belief on change, true change? He'd call it fifty-fifty out loud, but in his brain, no way, José. They could grow, gain more experience. But there were certain things just embedded in their DNA. He'd probably hate for someone to say that about him, if they had some kind of problem. He was a damn hypocrite. Shit, who wasn't?

Fenton got home and passed out. When he awoke, the sun was in descent. He got up and looked in the fridge but there wasn't anything in there except a bottle of mustard and a lemon. He put on some fresh clothes, brushed his teeth, and went to the grocery store.

He was walking down the aisle with a basket and around the corner came Pearson and his new wife, a petite brunette who, on paper, was perfect for him. Who knew what life was like for them behind closed doors, but to the public they seemed very appropriate.

"Hey y'all," Fenton said, unable to disappear into thin air thus accepting the unavoidable interaction.

"Hey, Fenton," Pearson said, a pained look on his face.

"I've been wanting to talk to you, Fenton," his wife said. The way she said it, her body seemed to charge up. Like she had porcupine quills sprout from her back. Fenton immediately felt in danger. "You're not going out with my husband anymore."

"Excuse me?" he said.

"Guess where I found him last night?"

Fenton looked at Pearson, then back at her. "Where?"

"On the sidewalk, on his back, passed out. I woke up and saw he wasn't in bed and freaked out. I was this close to calling the police. Instead, I went outside, just to see if there was any trace of him. I found him that way. Just passed out on the street. Can you imagine if our neighborhood was dangerous and someone had come across him that way? I had to basically pull him into the house. When he could finally say anything intelligent, he told me you got him wasted last night."

Fenton looked at Pearson again. The man looked even more sorry this time, but he didn't say anything. It was like Fenton could see him shrinking right before his eyes. It disgusted Fenton. He looked back at the man's wife.

"I can't have my husband passed out on the street, Fenton. Do you understand that? I can't lose him. You guys are grown men. It was a Wednesday for Christ's sake."

"It won't happen again. I promise," Fenton told her. "I'm truly very sorry."

"You're really going to have to grow up, Fenton. When you have a lady at home, she won't allow this from you either. It's selfish behavior and it's reckless and it's dangerous."

"You're absolutely right. I gotta clean up my act."

"I hope that you do. Let's go, Pearson."

She walked past Fenton, and Pearson followed, not a word. Fenton smiled as he went by.

Alone again in the aisle, he looked down into his basket. There were only a few items in there, none that required refrigeration. He hadn't gotten to that part yet. He put the basket on the floor and left the grocery store. He got into his car and drove to a bar where his buddy was working. Everybody called his buddy the Rain.

"Hey there, hoss," he greeted Fenton. "How you feeling?"

"Like riding the lightning. Y'all still got those wings in the back?"

"You bet."

"I'm gonna make an order, I'm starving. In the meantime, set me up."

"Whoo, boy," the Rain said, grinning.

Fenton came back with a number he placed on the bar. Awaiting him was a sweating bottle of the champagne of beers and a lustrous shot of whiskey. The Rain was holding his own shot aloft. Fenton sat down, picked up the glass and they clinked them together.

HE'S A LOT OF FUN

"So this is what I'm going to do. I'm going to fly to Italy. Stay there for a month. I'm going to work at a butcher's shop. Like really mom and pop. I'm going to learn everything they can teach me. I'm going to take all that knowledge and come back here and open my own butcher shop. But we'll serve food too. We'll make sandwiches. Delicious sandwiches. Maybe ice cream too. I gotta talk to Jay about his ice cream idea. Have you heard his idea about ice cream? It's great. It's the best idea. It's like nothing this town's seen. I mean, this town, there's still so much you can do here. Do you guys need a drink? I'm gonna get one. I'll be right back."

We just sat there, Liesl and I, smiling politely, as Rooster got up without waiting for us to answer and headed over to the counter to order another Lone Star. I watched his jerky movement. His jawline clenched in the moments he wasn't talking, which were seldom.

"He like this all the time now?" I asked her quietly, kind of embarrassed.

"At night. When we're out with everyone. In the day, when it's just us, it's about his plans of coming to visit me and that he's over being in this town. That we'll be together again. This whole future. Like his Italy dream, but with me in it."

"God," I was shaking my head.

She continued to smile. As if we were waiting in line at a

supermarket. Completely composed. That seemed to me a very southern attribute. A learned level of class and grace. I knew she was sad. But there wasn't a whole lot I could do. I was still unwittingly focused on him.

"It's going to be hard for him for a while," I said.

"For me too," Liesl said, as if to finally remind me, everyone. I felt a wave of guilt. What a jerk I was being. This was her going away party.

I wondered briefly how much I'd missed all along. I never wanted to see other people's problems, I realized. When I did, I knew it was time to go. But that wasn't what I was doing this time. I knew that much. Maybe that's what it looked like, but I knew that's not what it was.

"I'm sorry, Liesl."

"It's OK." She was still smiling. Her eyes seemed infinitely patient, but I knew that couldn't be possible, not even for her.

At the counter, other friends had joined Rooster. They laughed, ordered whiskey, lit cigarettes. There was a chill breeze. It seemed unusual, this time of year in Austin. In a month's time, I'd be gone too.

We watched him a while, both of us silent. Maybe we were both already far away.

"You know . . . a lot of people would always say how alike he and I are," I said. "Hanging out all the time. We laugh all the time. We got a lot in common, right? But as the days get closer," I shook my head, suddenly finding it hard to speak, "I think we just always had a lot of fun together."

"Yeah. I think that's it, Levy. He's a lot of fun. It's what we all love about him."

SUPER SUNDAY

It was early afternoon and I walked into the darkness of Parasol's like it was the velvety wing of a bat inviting me inside forever. I took a stool at the counter of the bar. There was only one other man in there. He had a big gray beard and he sat at the end of the bar and didn't look my way at all. He was wearing a denim vest and a T-shirt underneath and I could see a tattoo on his arm that looked faded, like a flag left out in the rain. The lady bartending came up to me. She was built like a football player. She was from England. She'd originally come to America to be a singer. Seemed like it hadn't really worked out but some nights you could catch glimpses of her dream when the bar was packed and the drinks were flowing and she put a tune in the juke that she liked.

"What are you having?" she asked me.

"Can you put a shot of tequila in a pint glass for me, fill it with ice, and then pour a Stiegl Radler on top?"

She took a moment to process the instructions, then nodded and did so. She left the can next to the glass, still a quarter of the Austrian grapefruit beer left. I took the first sip and it was exactly what I wanted. I hadn't yet taken the second sip when the door came open again. A block of sunlight with it.

In came Indy. He walked over and the way he walked reminded me of how a man whose employment was hard labor might walk. Heavy steps, and in no rush. I stood up from my stool and turned to him and we put our arms around each other, patting each other on the back gruffly, not to indicate we were tough but more to show we were present and grateful. He took a seat. The bartender stood there watching us with no expression.

"I'll have a Guinness," Indy said.

She went off to pour. It would take a while. It was a Guinness. We looked at each other.

"How are you?" I asked.

"I'm hanging in there."

"Yeah?"

"Work is killing me."

"It's a lot, huh? Being the boss?"

"All the time."

"Shit," I said.

His Guinness arrived and we cheersed. We took a sip and basked in the silence of the bar. There was a television on but no sound. The captions played. The movie was *Starship Troopers*.

"An excellent film," Indy said.

"Would you say underrated?" I asked.

"I think it's rated exactly right."

"Ha," I said. We both stared at the screen. Without looking away, I asked, "You guys get affected much by Mardi Gras?"

"I thought it would keep everyone away from the restaurant, but I was wrong."

"That's a good thing," I said.

"Eh. It can be a little much. And we have no way to predict anything. It's tricky."

"I can see that, I guess. You got any plans to get out there?"

"We're shutting down Fat Tuesday. That'll be the day me and Becca go for it."

"I'll be out there," I took a long pull from my drink. "Hey, you ever go to Super Sunday?"

Indy chuckled. "Nah, man. 'Less I get invited, I sit out on that one."

"Why's that?" I asked, looking over at him now.

Indy sighed and smiled sardonically. "To put it simply, that party isn't meant for me. And I can respect that. Everything doesn't have to be for me. Contrary to popular belief, a white guy in America isn't entitled to every event on this Earth."

I laughed. The bartender craned her neck to me for a second with a lifted eyebrow, then went back to the paperback she had her nose into.

"That's damn enlightened of you to say so, Indy. I feel like that's the first time I've heard a white guy say that out loud."

"You should hear the things I don't say out loud. Better yet, good thing you can't."

■

Mardi Gras came and went in New Orleans and I'd only had my bike stolen. For others, the toll extracted had been far worse.

The hustlers were especially good this year. I'd heard on one stretch of St. Charles, in the Lower Garden District, they'd pick-pocketed seven women's phones all in a row, all standing next to each other. One of the girls, going to check her Instagram, started hollering her phone was gone and one by one, right down the line, they all discovered the same. You almost had to admire it.

But finally, it was Super Sunday, almost as fun for me as Fat Tuesday itself. I hadn't been in a couple of years though, so I was especially looking forward to it. I'd gotten up early and was making my way over, walking with a cup full of Prosecco and topped with some satsuma I'd juiced. The weather was brisk but the sun was out. I crossed St. Charles and wove my way into Central City. I noticed people walking in the same direction in pairs or small groups. All different ages. But nearly all of them white. I didn't think much of it. I finally got to Washington Avenue and started to walk north. Things had definitely changed since I'd lived up the block. I was happy to see a big new Red Zone convenience store but a surprising number of houses had become renovated. They had banners hanging or nice wicker rocking chairs on their porches. By then, I was walking in the middle of the street and the amount of people walking along with me had grown dramatically. The crowd had diversified but I was still surprised by how many white people there were. There were a lot. More than I'd ever seen for the historic Super Sunday. Ahead, I could hear the drums of the Mardi Gras Indians.

The police had put up some orange barricades to prevent vehicles from going up Washington any further. Some black folk still angled their motorcycles through the barricades to line up with the others across LaSalle. Their motorcycles were very colorful, often with images spray painted on. It could be an image of a family member or just someone they admired. On one I remembered seeing the portrait of Sho'nuff from *The Last Dragon*. Another, Lil Wayne. Weezy F. Baby. Please say the Baby.

I passed by the shitty apartment complex I had first lived in when I'd moved to New Orleans, so many years ago. Didn't know a damn thing about the city back then besides what *Treme* had shown me on HBO and what I'd heard from the 504 Boyz on the radio. I don't know if *Easy Rider* counted. I knew *Interview with the Vampire* didn't.

The parking lot still looked bombed out, concrete broken and jutting like the smashed teeth in the mouth of a beggar. I remembered standing outside my door on the second floor, looking over. That day I'd heard the drums of the Indians, having no idea what a Super Sunday was. No clue how close I was to such a cultural phenomenon, and one of the last in this fading country...

■

That day, I slid a shirt over my head and put on a cap and went out into the streets. There were black people everywhere, the most I'd ever seen in my life, seemingly sprouted from the Earth, sitting in lawn chairs, smoking cigarettes, giving each other handshakes, drinking tall boys in paper bags, grilling off the back of their trucks, selling liquor and hot sausage po' boys and even an opportunity to a porta-potty. Music blasting from speakers that stood taller than me. Black people dancing, laughing, wearing their best and flashiest clothes. Crawfish shells littered the streets like abandoned rubies. The streets were completely full. And wherever a mob congregated, in the center you could find the Indians, battling.

Of course, this had been going on long before I'd been born. This was tradition, borne from things not so romantic or pretty. Borne from necessity, and the passion and love of men's hearts. Back in a time when they were still viewed as hostile. Still dangerous. Tribal, primal. Because back in the day of its inception, these black and brown men were only onto themselves. And being alone, they had to focus and concentrate their creativity and wishes, for better things, or else the cycle was endless massacre. A full year, a family coming together, constructing these gorgeous outfits.

Their feathers and crests poked above the heads of the people surrounding them, bobbing up and down. Their chants in some language I couldn't immediately translate. Their movements seemed animalistic to me, aggressive, showy. This was intentional. And even more, you could listen to their words. This was a real language. The words had meant something. They were foreign to me, but I could tell by how passionately they were chanted, the gravity of their implication. And the costumes. So beautiful. It was really like some scene from a documentary, except this was real life. Was and wasn't. I could get so close. See the beads of sweat on their noses, only their faces exposed, a story emblazoned on their chests, a history, a future. It was intoxicating, thrilling, forcing me to bend my knees, stomp my feet. I laughed, my eyes closed, clapping my hands with the beat of the drums.

■

That was so many years ago. The drums and the speakers and the chants, they all seemed muffled that present day. On the sidewalks, in the median, sitting, staring, their phones bared, filming everything, were white people. It caused me to stop dead in my tracks. They were everywhere. And they were ecstatic to be there. They pointed at the Indian families marching down LaSalle, drinking beer they'd stored in their backpacks, sitting on their Mexican style serape blankets, documenting everything on their phones. This would all be displayed on their social media, of course. This was exciting. No other city in America could boast such an event. Out here in the streets. They'd captured it all. They were witnesses.

There were still black people out there, many of them, but it was almost as if they had taken a back seat to the white people, standing against buildings, sitting on stoops and ledges, maybe a look of despondency, muted integrity, discreet confusion. The native folk had taken a backseat, and none of them appeared surprised by a damn sight.

I was getting this sick feeling. I stood there, watching the oblivious tourists watching the black people, none of them ever actually intermingling, none of them talking to each other. A family of Indians were making their way down the street, and an older white woman with a puffy Patagonia vest stepped in front of them, causing the family to pause, so she could take a selfie with them. I looked at the little daughter's beautiful face, framed in the bright feathers and intricate stitching, her drooping full lips, sulking shoulders, her eyes revealing her sad heart. There should have been fire there. It killed me not to see it. The older white woman got her picture and rejoined her delighted and tragically unaware ranks, the lot of them immediately inspecting the quality of the shot, chortling in delightfully.

The sick feeling began to gradually replace itself with anger. The anger surprised me. I didn't feel I had a right to feel angry. This wasn't my birthplace. These weren't my people. I had no family out here. I only just knew, in my heart of hearts, this wasn't right. A friend spotted me from the sea of people, a coworker.

"Fenton!" she called out to me, waving. Her auburn hair glittered in the sunlight. She was with two other girls. Their expressions seemed a little nervous but still enthusiastic. I waved back weakly but couldn't change my face, and I didn't really want to, so I chose to walk away.

I was thinking bad things, bad words. I knew my face had become dark and cold. Ugly. I wanted to look unapproachable. I'd only been there for fifteen minutes and I found I couldn't take it. I left the crowds, on the verge of muttering things. I passed blocks, and the crowd began to thin, and eventually, I was alone again, deep in Central City, where the streets were narrow and the concrete jagged and the arches of the houses sagged, where the grass was uncut and the parked cars were missing hubcaps and side mirrors and mattresses lay in vacant lots with messages spray painted across them.

Steadily, my negative and violent urges began to dissipate. I could feel the temperature behind my temples cooling. I was able to breathe regularly and I felt peace return to me.

It surprised me to have such a strong reaction. To have those vicious thoughts. I wasn't from here. Who was I to be indignant? Well, even if I wasn't from here, I wasn't white either. So what does that mean? I thought about the idea of voyeurism. I could understand what the positions were. I think that little girl in the Indian family could too. But I thought about something else too. Something I didn't know a word for. I remembered living in the suburbs briefly during middle school. I was looking inside a car parked next door to where my family lived. There was a large stuffed shark in the backseat. I heard a man's voice behind me.

"Can I help you?"

I turned to see a tall white man with a rigid haircut standing there, his hands on his hips. His expression was very severe, I remembered. I felt embarrassed for some reason, and I tried to explain myself without stuttering. I was a kid.

"I was just looking at the shark," I said meekly.

He just stared at me, frowning, not saying anything, so I walked away, feeling a shame I couldn't rationalize. I went back into my house, but I remember never feeling safe in that suburb. Always feeling any time I walked down the street that there could be a million eyes on me. Feeling as if I were in perpetual danger, even though the streets were the cleanest nicest streets I'd ever walked down.

PUGNACIOUS

"See, that's your problem. You don't like to listen. I tell you something and you think you know better. But that's the thing, Chael. You don't. You don't know better. How could you? You just started. So what do we do here? 'Cause you don't want to listen, and you don't know better but you are still doing whatever you want to do and the whole night tanks. You fuck us. That's what you do. You fuck us. 'Cause of what?"

Chael was taller than me but at that moment I was looming over him. To his credit, he'd kept eye contact the entire time. That wasn't an easy thing to do. He'd been scolded before. Maybe he would for his entire life.

"Tell me," he said.

"Your ego. You're a kid and you got too much ego. What's the sign in the back say? "Focus or fuck us." You need to learn to listen, Chael. You're gonna learn here or you're going to keep fucking up until you learn somewhere else. Why not learn sooner than later?"

"I'd like to," he said.

"Then fucking listen," I said and cuffed him on the back of his blond-haired head. I understood perfectly well, somewhere else, something like that would get me fired. I didn't even like being this type of teacher. I'd gone through many versions before this. I'd tried nice. I'd tried encouraging. I'd tried silent angry body language. I'd even just stood in front of him and asked him what the problem was. He just answered, "What do you mean?"

So here we were with the crack-the-whip, tough-love older brother routine. I was desperate to make this thing work. It was getting to a point where it might come down to me or him if we didn't. I still had faith. Because at least he kept eye contact.

We went about our business. People left the restaurant. We started closing down the bar. As I was wiping down the bar, Chael said cheerfully, "Get a drink tonight?"

I stopped what I was doing and looked at him skeptically, "I don't think so."

I didn't say that because I didn't want to get a drink. I was assuredly leaving this place to get several. But I also knew it was the start of a long week. I needed to reserve my energy, patience, and fortitude. And I didn't care if that hurt the young man's feelings. He'd get over it.

That week was as brutal as any other. But we made it. We lived. Like I'd always had. Like I always would. Chael had only been half bad. He was getting better in some ways. But that last night, Saturday night, there was some controversy on the kitchen's end.

"Quentin's getting the boot," I said dryly, my arms crossed as I watched our main dishwasher rumble out of the restaurant with a slew of expletives in his wake.

"That sucks," Chael said. "But it doesn't affect us."

I cocked my head at him sharply. "Doesn't affect us?" I repeated.

"Well, that's back of the house," he said.

"Let me tell you something, you little shit. This is a restaurant. We ALL work here. Just because Q wasn't back here polishing our glasses or getting us ice doesn't mean his absence won't hurt us. Missing him will put a bigger strain on the kitchen. That means that could affect the time it takes for food to get out. That means dishware could run low. That means they will be more stressed out and when you're stressed out you can make more mistakes. We're not just making drinks for this whole restaurant, we're serving food too. Plus, those are our friends, right? Do you think they look over at us when we are getting buried and say, "Oh it doesn't affect us?" No. They watch on with sympathy and say goodbye kindly to us at the end of the night. Maybe they make us extra food for the end of the night. We're all in this together, Chael. You don't just look over to some other part of the room and say "Oh well, I'm standing over here. Fuck off." We're a team. And if one end is hurting, we all hurt."

Chael was looking down at his shoes. When he finally looked up, he had his hands on his hips. "You're right. That was selfish of me. I feel bad it's going to hurt them tonight. Hurt us."

I walked away from him, shaking my head.

The night went on. Service went full steam ahead. I didn't have any time to even look at my cellphone, we were so busy. I didn't have time to look at the kitchen either. But they made it and we made it and everybody did the best they could. Chael and I stood by the short dish washer machine we had behind the bar, loading a rack up with glasses.

"What's the main difference between when I train you and when Gina does?" I asked him in a much gentler tone than previously that night.

"Gina's like a patronizing schoolteacher. You're like a drill sergeant," he told me.

I liked that.

An hour before we closed, his little brother came and sat at the bar. He'd come with a date. I said hello and good to see you but nothing beyond that. Their noses were so turned up, that was the extent of the effort I was going to be able to muster that night and make it to close in one piece. I knew Chael came from money and had no business working in this restaurant, but I was surprised to see him nervous at this point of the night. Out of sorts. We'd already gotten through the hard push. He was fucking up simple things. Knocking over glasses. I walked over to him.

"Chill out and get your shit together," I said under my breath, but very close to his ear.

"OK," he answered, his blue eyes bobbing in their sockets.

It was after service and we were wiping and polishing our stations. I stood up straight from the well.

"You were nervous making drinks in front of your brother."

"Why would I be nervous? It's just my little brother."

"Uh-huh," I said.

"You got brothers?" Chael asked me after a while.

"Oh yeah."

"How many?"

"Three."

"Where are you?"

"With my sister, included?" I said. "Exact middle."

"Exact middle?"

"Yeah," I said.

"That explains a lot."

"What's it explain, Chael?"

"Why you're so pugnacious and hungry."

"Hell yeah," I grunted.

I finished polishing a glass and went into the back. Jerry was there, looking at his phone. I liked Jerry. I came up behind him. He was swiping through a dating app.

"He's cute," I said.

Jerry didn't turn around. "Too cute. I like them a little rugged," he told me.

"Yeah I bet you do," I laughed. Then I whispered, "The fuck does 'pugnacious' mean?"

"I don't know," he said, and seemed genuinely perplexed. Bothered, even. "Let me look it up."

I stood there waiting as he did.

He read it aloud from his phone. "Eager or quick to argue, quarrel, or fight."

I looked down, pursing my lips. Then I nodded.

"Yup," I said. I walked back to the bar. I put my hands on my hips. Chael looked up from wiping the drains on the bar.

"You did all right tonight. You only really fucked up at the end. Next week, I want you to work on keeping your station cleaner. This isn't your damn living room."

"Cleanliness is next to Godliness," he repeated one of my lines.

"Damn right. Now hurry up and let's get out of here," I said. "First one's on me."

TIGER

I woke up to a text message from my mother. It said, Hope you are taking care of yourself.

I got out of bed and went to the bathroom and flipped the switch for the light. The bathroom in the hotel room had one of those big mirrors that took up the whole wall. I'm not gonna lie, I was looking good naked. Haha.

Funny too, coming back to this city. And now, a totally different person. But I wasn't sure if I completely believed that. I wasn't sure if anyone else would either. So I never told anyone when I came back. I'd arrive unannounced and flit through the shadows and delight in the surprised exaltations of old friends who thought they were seeing a ghost. My sick pleasure.

I only ever told her. And who would've thunk it. This woman who all these years I'd thought was so far out of my league. Here, with me. And it was good. It was all good. My mind was changing. Maybe that's the kind of thing only women can see. The fairer sex.

I used the toilet, then I washed my hands, then I brushed my teeth. I came back into the room to see her on the edge of the bed, her bare back to me, brushing her long black hair. Beautiful hair, like it was the mane of some majestic animal you might admire and one day hope to befriend or even fall in love with. On her violin shaped back, a big tattoo of a tiger, baring its teeth and ripping red in her flesh.

"Feel like getting a bite?" I asked.

"I gotta go to work."

"OK," I said.

I went back into the bathroom. Not for any particular reason. I guess this was sort of the awkward morning after. Still, it was cool I could pay for a hotel room by myself now and have a beautiful woman keep me company. I'd take a shower and make myself coffee and see where the day took me.

And as if she had been reading my mind, she called from the other room, "What are you gonna do today?"

I walked back into the room. "I don't know. Run around. Maybe go to jail or something."

She was just shimmying her jeans up over her hips. I paused in the door to watch. I thought to myself, no matter where or what or when, moments like these will never get old.

She turned after she'd buttoned up. She crossed her arms. "God, I'm tired of dudes like you."

"Dudes like me? You never known a dude like me," I said. Like it was reflex. And I regretted it instantly, because I knew, to her, how phony it sounded.

She let me have it.

"I've known plenty of dudes like you. Just like you. Hey, listen, buster. You ain't some spring chicken anymore. Dudes like you, you live so damn self-destructive. You fashion yourself some real tough fuckers, huh? Fuck this. Fuck that. Here for a good time, not for a long time. Thinking any moment's gonna be your last." She said all this smiling. It made me smile too, like an idiot. "Next thing you know, you find yourself going into your thirties and you're still here. Except now you got bad knees or bad credit or less hair or a gut. That really the destiny you got mapped out for yourself, handsome?"

No one had ever talked to me like that before. As in, envisioned a future for me. A future I might be successful in. No one but me. And myself? I'd only done it in glimpses, in the hypothetical form. A night where the stars might be clear in the sky. I stood there, speechless.

"You wanna come down to the lobby with me? Get some coffee?"

"Yeah. I do. Let me put some clothes on."

I did that and we walked to the door. Then I remembered. "Oh wait, I gotta put my shoes on too."

"Don't rush," she said. "Have a seat in that nice chair. Put them on one at a time."

REAL LIFE

Eldridge wasn't a very articulate sort of fellow. But he was a guy people trusted. Some people. And the trust might not have come easy but when it arrived, it was as real as anything you could say was real. As real as the grass was green, as real as this month's rent. When you asked him a question, his face looked like it went deep into thought. He looked down at the floor. He pursed his lips. The way his face was made, his expression could get pretty dark, and that didn't just mean his complexion. A lot of times, the answer would only ever be a word or two. It wasn't uncommon for people to mistake him for being simple. A lot of people were dipshits.

His good friends called him El. That night, he was at work, just not on the clock. He was having a drink at the bar. He liked his place of employment, even when he wasn't working. It was just his kind of bar. He thought the counter was beautiful, and it was the kind of dark that fit with his face. Made him not look so scary to the people that liked bright places. You know, people who liked to jog with their dogs or fly kites. The bar made him look like he belonged. Like maybe he was supposed to be there. Funny how we all want to belong even when so many times we don't.

He sat alone at the end of the bar, taking his time on a rum old-fashioned. His coworker Tito came up from the other side of the counter, a dish rag over his shoulder. Eldridge liked Tito very much. Always had. Tito was flashy in some ways, but he was quiet a lot of the time too. He was good with his hands and quick to smile, kind of a goofy guy, but a good heart, and Eldridge had fostered a special fondness for his coworker, a loyalty the way he did for his closest friends, and he never wanted to see Tito unhappy, even though he had been a bit somber as of late.

"What do you got for your night off, El?"

"No plans."

"Pretty cool art show on O.C. Haley. You oughta check it out."

"Oh yeah?"

"It's only a handful of blocks from here. The weather's perfect. Take a drink to go and check it out for me."

"OK, Tito."

Eldridge got a double daiquiri to go. It was a sweet time of year in New Orleans. Just after Mardi Gras, and Eldridge's pockets were fat. He strolled leisurely in the middle of the street with his plastic cup, taking sips and raising his hand to people who passed by, and they returned his greeting with smiles and nods. Though he was a private person, moments like these, which were thankfully many in this town, were plentiful, and no one had to know him, and he didn't have to know anyone. They could all just be grateful for this place and their life, money or no money, just that good sliver of freedom to walk down a street with a drink in hand and music in the air.

He took a left onto O.C. Haley and sure enough the art show was just a couple blocks up. People were spread out on the sidewalk, their own to-go cups in hand, and just above them, the night sky was on its unhurried descent, the horizon draped with a pink ribbon where the sun gave everyone a final and knowing wink for the day, though it would assuredly crisp all our asses with searing judgment in the morning promised to come.

Eldridge walked up and as he was taking his time to finish his cocktail, he saw Tamara off to the side, talking to a tall man with very dark skin, glasses and dreads bunched up on the top of his head. Almost immediately, he caught Tamara's eye. He walked over in no rush and smiled. She paused in her conversation and the tall man did too and they both looked at Eldridge.

"Hi, Tam," Eldridge said.

"Hey El," Tamara said, smiling awkwardly. She looked at the tall man and then introduced them. Eldridge shook the man's hand, still smiling, looking up at him, into his eyes through his glasses, almost immediately forgetting his name.

"I'm gonna talk to my friend a minute, cool if I catch up to you?" Tamara asked her friend. He did something weird with his lips, maybe it was supposed to be an expression of limp affirmation, then he turned around, looking for someone else to talk to, somewhere else to be. Eldridge and Tamara walked down the sidewalk a bit, a few steps away from the crowd.

"How you holding up?" Eldridge asked her.

"I'm doing great. I'm busy, I got a lot going. I feel like the wind is under my arms. My wings. I feel good."

"I'm glad to hear that," Eldridge told her.

"How is he?"

"Well, he's pretty sad," Eldridge told her.

"Really?"

"Yeah. He's pretty beat up. He puts on a good face, but he's pretty beat up."

"I mean, Tito's gotta get back out there. A big part of the problem for us was he would get so bogged down. Too much work. We weren't LIVING. We're still young! I want to go places, do things! You know what I mean, El?"

"I do. I know it."

"He'll get over it."

"Yeah."

"You here for the art show?"

"Yeah. Was Tito who actually told me about it. Said I should check it out. My night off and all."

"Well. He always had good taste."

"True. Guess I'll go check it out. Good to see you, Tam."

"Oh, El," she said to him, wrapping her arms around his neck. He bent down to give her a proper hug. Then he smiled again and walked into the gallery. The art was fine. They had free wine and some cheese in there. The food truck outside was serving Caribbean. The jerk chicken was amazing.

■

Weeks later, Eldridge and Tito had scheduled a Thursday off together to see Kamasi Washington in the Quarter at One Eyed Jacks. Eldridge wasn't a big jazz guy but his neighbor had gifted him the tickets for a problem Eldridge had helped him out with. His neighbor did photography for bands on the side of his day gig, but sometimes there'd be some jerk who'd request commission and then didn't want to pay after the job. That's when his neighbor would ask Eldridge to accompany him to ask for the money in person. That usually solved the problem. They usually always got the money. In some way or another.

Tito and Eldridge were in line for the venue and Tito was telling him about the new girl he'd met. Eldridge could tell Tito was pretty excited about the girl and that made Eldridge happy, because he genuinely liked to see his friends happy. He might be suspicious when he finally actually met the other person but that was between him and the other person, at the moment he could visibly see how happy his friend was so he stayed quiet and kept a smile on his face and let his buddy gush about this new girl.

"She's going to school to be a doctor too," Tito said.

"Seems above your pay grade," Eldridge said. They both started laughing. "I can't wait to meet her," he told Tito.

"Thanks, El. Me too. She's really something," Tito said, putting his hand on Eldridge's shoulder.

Behind them, they heard a woman say with a loud voice, "I'm so fucking excited to see Kamasi in New Orleans. This will be historic."

The two of them turned around to see a white woman and the man she was with. It was as if the woman had been waiting for Tito and Eldridge to turn around. She had a bit of a frenzied look in her eyes. Eldridge turned around immediately without a word once he'd saw it, because he'd seen it before in his life and would probably see it many more times. Tito, being the southern gentleman that he was, smiled politely, nodded, then turned back around.

But the woman wasn't finished. Because of the courteous eye contact Tito had gifted her, the woman had taken this as an invitation, a gateway into their lives. She put a claw on Tito's shoulders and said, "You know he's supposed to be like the Otis Redding of our generation."

"No, I didn't know that," Tito said sheepishly. It was funny, to Eldridge anyway, because Tito was a musician, always played great music at the bar on the Spotify, and also, of course, he was black. Also. To boot. It became funny, as this woman began informing them about the Otis Redding of their generation. And in New Orleans. Eldridge felt a familiar murmur of heat beginning to prickle up his back. A primitive instinct that blinked red inside him.

"That's crazy you didn't know that," the woman continued. "He's from Inglewood, started in the clubs in Los Angeles. He's the future. We're all blessed to be able to witness him tonight. I don't know if you know that yet. We're blessed," she said.

"Oh. OK," Tito said.

"God, I'm excited for you. I'm excited for all of us but especially for you. You're just walking into this. Wild. Did your friend get the tickets? I bet he knows all this."

"Yeah, he did get the tickets, actually," Tito said.

Eldridge knew that was a social cue to get involved. But that's where he was a little different from other people. Eldridge didn't turn around. He didn't look back or do anything at all. He remained completely still, even though it would be impossible to think he hadn't heard.

"I bet you know all about Kamasi, right?" she said behind Eldridge. "I mean, you have to. You just have to."

And that was the moment Eldridge chose to turn around. Then. And when he turned around, he turned all the way around. He faced her completely. His face had become dark like it did sometimes, in the bars, in the bodegas, on the street, behind the cars and in the allies. Eldridge's secret power that was so many white people's darkest fear. The sheer exhibition of his black skin and his terrifying dismay with their oblivious intrusion into a world that is not their own.

"Why do I have to?" Eldridge asked the woman, his voice raised only one octave. "Tell me why I have to know. Tell me."

The woman reared back a little bit, more definitive to her true nature, and her man was there behind her, and he put his arms around her protectively, also instinctively. They went quiet, acutely and ashamedly aware of the situation they'd now found themselves, staring at Eldridge, then down at their feet, like they were little kids being sent to the corner. Except there was no corner. There was no place to go and close your eyes. This was real life. And they'd were looking right at it. Eldridge stayed like that a while, even if the line may have been moving behind him.

Then he looked at Tito. Tito was grinning at him. Eldridge took the tickets out of his pockets and ripped them in quarters. He tossed them on the slick sidewalk. The couple and the folks in line watched in horror.

"Fuck this place. Let's go get drunk," Eldridge said. They both stepped out of line and started walking up the street, towards Decatur. They didn't look back once. Tito put his arms on Eldridge's shoulders, laughing.

■

Eldridge was on his phone, laying on his back in bed, checking Facebook one afternoon. He was just killing time before work. He wasn't a big social media guy, he really wasn't a big anything kind of guy. He'd always sort of done things in moderation. Some things maybe a little more than moderation. Maybe much more. But only when the situation called for it. He could enjoy a nice steak out at a restaurant. He could be just as happy sitting at home and eating a can of black beans. All you had to do was season those suckers. He could sit at a bar by himself and have a few cocktails. He could be somewhere, packed bar, chugging a beer faster than his boss any night of the week. And his boss was Irish. A Patriots fan. Eldridge liked him anyway, somehow.

He'd gotten a friend request from an old classmate. It was nice. Looked like his buddy had had two kids. Seemed appropriate. He knew his buddy would make a good dad. Eldridge could tell that all the way back in middle school.

He started scrolling down his public feed, dragging his finger down the screen of the phone. That's where he saw a post from Tamara. Eldridge read the post. "Oh man," he said to himself.

Tamara must've found out Tito was going with his new girl.

She was lighting him up. And it wasn't just the one post. Eldridge looked on her page now. There were nasty words all over the place. It was awful, and it made Eldridge feel terrible. He felt terrible because he didn't understand what it was for. The end of a relationship could hurt. Yeah. But all this? She was saying all these ugly things about Tito. But, supposedly, she'd gotten over him so fast, she'd broken up with him, so why all this? It didn't make sense to Eldridge. She'd always made it seem like it was his problem. She told everyone that. But now there was all this. Nasty things. About how he'd been while they dated, about what she thought now, about how she felt betrayed, even though they'd been broken up almost half a year. She was even saying nasty things about how Tito looked. That was the most ridiculous part. Everyone knew Tito was a handsome guy. Maybe not the best dresser. He was an all right dresser. The main thing was, he was handsome. So what if he had curly hair? Didn't everyone like curls?

Eldridge focused on the curly hair part because there was someone constantly posting on each of Tamara's disparaging posts, and the person had a comment to say about Tito's appearance. He compared him to some corny R&B star, which still wasn't much of an insult, because that star had had some legitimate hits. Some legitimate baby-making hits. But still, Eldridge thought it was in poor taste. It was a cheap attack. All of it was hard to read. He cared a lot about Tamara and Tito both. He felt bad Tamara was hurting, but still, he wondered, why all this all of a sudden? He'd met them both when they were still together. They'd both been very important to him. Maybe he was closer to Tito now because he worked with Tito, but he still cared very deeply for Tamara. It made him feel awful to see this, all of it out there for everyone to see on the internet. It was so ugly. When did the world get like this?

Eldridge left a comment. Something very simple. One of those emojis. Eldridge wasn't much for words. He didn't want to get involved at all, really. But he felt obligated in some unexplainable way. He had to express himself. He commented an emoji. The un-smiley face.

Not even two minutes went by and he got a notification on his phone. Someone had commented on the emoji he'd left behind. Eldridge looked at the comment. It read: "Why you butthurt?"

It was the same person who had been commenting on all the other posts. Eldridge finally looked at the person's profile. He recognized who it was. He hadn't remembered the man's name at the time but there he was in front of him now. Asher. It was the tall guy Tamara had been talking to outside of the art show.

Eldridge knew it was dumb to get into things online. He knew it was futile. But this had to do with two friends of his. He knew he should've just got off his phone, got in the shower, got ready for work. What he did anyway was comment back: "Don't fuck with me. These are friends of mine. I don't know you. And trust me, I ain't the one."

Funny how these things worked. That person, right there, in their living room, bedroom, place of work, in the driver's seat of their car in the parking lot of a grocery store, their phone in hand, computer in front of them, able to respond right away, as if it were a real conversation, real time. It wasn't. It wasn't real. Because if it were real, people would act like it was real. They'd consider the consequences. The consequences staring them right in the face.

This person, on the other side of a computer screen or phone screen, somewhere, on this Earth, commented again. "Who's this sad boy, Tamara? A friend of yours?"

And not five minutes went by that Tamara responded. It said, "He was. Until he chose the boy's club."

Eldridge read that, looking at the screen for a long while before he put it away. His heart felt heavy in his chest, like someone had put an anvil in his chest, with a note taped on it that said "Fuck you." He had to do a push up just to get out of bed. That second or however long it took, he had a hard time breathing. It didn't last that long, but it was a moment, a real crisp moment. Why'd she say that, he thought? Why'd she have to say that? He stood in the shower, long minutes, thinking about it. Finally, he turned the shower off. His phone glowed with another comment. It was from the same person, the third person.

"Don't cry, internet tough guy," the comment said.

Eldridge stared at the comment. He went to the profile and memorized the man's face. Then he put his phone down. He knew there wasn't anything else to do. It didn't matter how upset he was. There wasn't anything else to do. Not on the internet.

■

Summer was ending. That didn't mean the heat quit in New Orleans. But it wasn't so bad out that night. Not if you were used to it. Not if you liked it. Some people liked it. Eldridge and Tito were those kinds of people. Eldridge was stepping out of Tito's house. They'd just had dinner. Him, Tito, and Tito's girl. The new one. Only she wasn't so new anymore. They stood on the porch, Tito and El, post dinner.

Eldridge walked out to the edge of the porch, just up to the steps, and turned around. Tito was smiling. Eldridge started smiling too. He looked out sidewise, out into the street, at nothing.

"Well?" Tito asked.

"Yeah," Eldridge said.

They both laughed. Eldridge stepped forward and hugged Tito. Tito hugged him back.

"What you gonna do now?" Tito asked him.

"Go home."

"Bull."

"OK. Grab a quick drink and go home."

"Where?"

"I'm thinking Verret's."

"Oh my," Tito said. "You trying to get in there, huh?"

"Just real fast. Promise. In and out."

"Be safe."

They hugged again.

"I'm so happy for you," Eldridge said.

"It means a lot to me," Tito said back.

Eldridge smiled, giving Tito a look over his shoulder. Then he nodded, walking off the porch and out into the street and into his car.

He took Broad all the way into Central City and made a left onto Washington Avenue. He took that all the way straight to Verret's. He parked, tapped the button on his keys to make sure he locked it up, twice, and walked into the bar. Red light, tables spread out, music just right. Earth, Wind & Fire in the speakers. "Devotion." Like he was meant to walk in there. There were about three people at the bar. A couple and another man as fat as a hippo who used to be the door guy. The bar had let him go but still let him come by and drink for free. And then the bartender, completely indifferent to probably any subject in the world that didn't contribute to her modest way of life, which was all she wanted. To get along. Nothing more, nothing less. God bless you, momma. How rare a flower you are.

Eldridge sat at the bar and ordered a High Life and a shot of whiskey. She poured it all the way up. He said, "Whew."

"We take care of you, boo," the bartender said, winking with her eye and the gold tooth in her smile.

"I know you do, momma."

Eldridge took the shot back. It felt like he'd put back a bolt of lightning. It sparked him all the way down. He had to kick the bar. He felt embarrassed. The bartender laughed. All she wanted in life was for people to be happy. A rare sweet flower.

The couple at the other end of the bar turned to look at him. He looked at them apologetically initially. Then he recognized one of them. The man. The tall man. With the dreads on top of his head. Glasses. It was really him. Eldridge stared at him a second longer than he meant to. But he had to make sure. Then he turned back forward, calm, stoic, his High Life glistening into the electric future.

He stayed that way a long time. He became still. A statue. A Central City gargoyle. Perched. Waiting. He was waiting. Eldridge sipped his glowing High Life gingerly. He made everything he did slow motion. No one could see his mind. No one could see where it was going.

Eldridge didn't bother to see who the tall man was with. He only recognized when she got up to go to the bathroom, and the tall man was alone. Eldridge stood up and walked over. He tapped him rudely on the shoulder.

"Hey," Eldridge said.

The tall man turned around. He adjusted his glasses. Eldridge knew the guy wanted to act like he didn't recognize him, except he had already betrayed that when Eldridge had walked into the bar. You never mistake that flash in someone's eyes. Even if you don't recognize them, you understand, they recognize you, they know you from some place, some time. Where you did something. You could see it in the body language. It was there. They remembered. They'd never forgotten.

"Asher, right? You're Tamara's friend," Eldridge said. He didn't present it as a question.

The tall man didn't say anything. He stared at Eldridge from his glasses. He had nice lips. Big. They were open, and his eyes watched to see what Eldridge was going to say next.

"I met you on O.C. Haley. I was Tamara's friend too. Once. We don't talk anymore unfortunately. Don't like how that went. But life is life."

"I don't hardly talk to Tamara anymore either," the tall man said.

"Oh."

"We're not really friends."

"But still. You said what you said."

"What?" he said.

"You said what you said. About my friend. My friend Tito. The things you said on Facebook."

"Listen," the tall man said, standing up, looking down at Eldridge with his hands up to his chest. "I barely talk to Tamara anymore. We weren't great friends to begin with."

Eldridge's face remained deadpan, but he didn't move away. He stayed close to the tall man. "Then why'd you say those things? The things about my friend. You were insulting him. Then you insulted me. You called me an internet tough guy. Do you remember that?" Eldridge asked him.

The tall man's companion was returning from the bathroom. She had dirty blond hair and had a stud in her eyebrow. Eldridge could see it in the ruby light. Walking towards them, she noticed her friend standing, his body language. How stiff and uncomfortable he was. Then she saw Eldridge. She read his body language too. Eldridge and the tall man looked at her briefly, then back at each other.

Eldridge punched the tall man in the stomach hard. It was a punch he was very familiar with, in a place he was very familiar with. He went right inside of the tall man. Just above the stomach and below the ribs. The man bent down and when he did, Eldridge took the back of his head and smashed it on the top of the bar three times. It went really fast, but it was incredibly loud. Eldridge could hear something crunch the wrong way the third time he smashed the man's head on counter. And when he let go, the tall man slumped to the floor as if whatever had been standing him up had been stolen. It almost looked silly, looking down at him. This tall guy, looking like a boiled noodle at his feet. There was a little blood on the bar and Eldridge's High Life had gotten knocked over. The bartender didn't say anything nor did the ex-doorman. That man didn't work there anymore. He just got to drink for free.

The tall man's blonde friend had both hands over her mouth. Eldridge reached into his pocket and put all the money he had onto the bar counter. He set his knocked-over beer bottle back up and put some beverage napkins over the spill.

"Sorry, momma," Eldridge said.

The bartender sighed and shrugged. Eldridge looked down once more at the tall man, laying there at his feet. Then he walked out of the place.

SEE ME

The middle school I went to was all black. I was only half. I can remember two white people. One Chinese boy. He was tough as hell. Big muscles for our grade. The white girl was hard too. Sharp nose. Sharp teeth. The white guy was quiet, but smart, a quick and discreet sense of humor. But he was very, very quiet, and I don't think he ever looked anyone in the eyes. So what can you really actually know about a person?

No one knew what the hell to call me. No one knew who or what I was. Sometimes, they would ask though. Only ever girls. The ones that thought I was cute.

"What is you?" this one black girl asked me, all flirty. She wore glasses and she was exceptionally developed for how young we all were. And she knew it.

"I'm mixed," I told her.

"Like a damn dog. A mutt," her boyfriend said, coming up behind her and putting his arm over her shoulder.

School finished up for the day. The kids flooded the buses. I sat somewhere in the middle, and I wore my dad's big headphones, the ones he'd use when he was playing guitar alone in the basement. I always thought he looked so cool, quiet, focused, in some different universe, away from us all. That's what I wanted.

I felt the seat move next to me and it was the cute girl from class, the one with the boyfriend. She was saying something.

I lifted one headphone. "Huh?"

"I said, what are you listening to?" she asked me.

I was afraid to let her listen but I knew it was too late. We were both here. I handed the headphones over to her. She put them on her head. She listened for a moment, staring at me with a lopsided smile on her face that made me feel embarrassed but happy at the same time. Like she was trying to tell me something, like she was figuring it out. And she was telling me, I SEE YOU.

She took the headphones off and handed them back to me.

"You're weird," she said to me, shaking her head.

"Yeah," I said.

■

I was running a little late to work. After class, I'd spent too much time talking to my professor. I guess we liked to shoot the shit that way. We both knew I had to get to my job and we both knew it didn't matter at all.

Once I got there and clocked in, I put my apron on up over my head and made sure my tie was straight. I pushed through the doors and walked behind the bar. The manager was absent, so I was in the clear. The two other bartenders, my coworkers, two white dudes, stood there, both of them arms crossed. I came up next to them and did the same thing with my limbs.

One of my coworkers had blond hair and the other one had brown hair. The one with the blond hair said, "Heard about you last night."

"Heard what from who?" I asked.

Blond Hair nodded to Brown Hair. Brown Hair grinned. I did too.

"You like trouble," Blond Hair said.

"Yeah," I said.

"Ain't no one I'd rather roll with," Brown Hair said.

I smiled at him because it made me feel good for him to say so. "Y'all ready for tonight?" I asked.

"Does a sawhorse have a wooden dick?" Blond Hair said.

Three black women sat at the bar. I couldn't tell their age, but they all wore professional attire. They looked smart and they sat up straight and their demeanor, to me, and I do mean to me, seemed to not demand but simply require nothing less than respect, and I felt that with no adverse agenda. It made me feel good to see them. They probably just got off work. Ready for a well-deserved drink. I was a bartender. I understood this stage in life.

"We all know you got this one, Levy," Blond Hair said to me, grinning.

I could tell Blond Hair meant this in a sweet way. That he thought, in his unknowable mind, he was doing me some kind of favor. That he thought he knew me. It was hard to keep my face straight. I looked at Brown Hair. Brown Hair wasn't smiling but he didn't say anything. He just looked at me. He had blue eyes. He had a baby face. But he wasn't a baby anymore. And I knew that he knew.

I nodded and walked up to the beautiful and respectable and professional black ladies who were probably just my age or maybe a little older, and I asked them how their day was, and what I could get them to drink. They smiled radiantly.

■

I was living in the worst apartment I'd ever lived in my whole life in New Orleans, my favorite city in the whole wide world. I was just off Washington and LaSalle. Trust me, it was bad. It was the kind of place where if you walk down the street at night, if you are not feeling the hair on the back of your neck, you are just that kind of animal that ain't meant for long in this world. But I wasn't that kind of animal. I was the other kind.

I was in my thirties. And I was meaner than when I was young, but I wasn't as angry. Figure that one out.

It was my day off. I only wanted to get drunk and play music in my shitty little studio apartment. Play it real loud. Cook weird stuff. Jerk off. Wonder about where my life was going. I wasn't depressed. I was romantic. I loved this shit. I could have a girl over here anytime I wanted. I told you, I was romantic, and so were they. Eternally.

There was a little bodega around the corner. I don't know if the family who ran it were Chinese or Korean or Vietnamese. Normally, I was good at stuff like that.

I got a six pack of Modelo, a fifth of Hornitos, a pack of Newports, and a three-piece of fried chicken.

The Asian woman behind the counter squinted at me. There was only an old black man behind me. He was cradling a forty of Colt 45 in his arms like it was his firstborn. He wasn't in a rush to be anywhere. He'd already been there before, after all. A million times. I turned back to the woman.

"I see it," she said in her accent, still squinting her eyes at me.

"See what?" I asked her, holding back a smile.

"Asian in you," she said, grinning now, like she'd caught me cheating.

I grinned too. I don't know why or how, but no matter where I went in the world, no matter what age I was, it was only Asian people who could see themselves in me. Only. And it forever endeared them to me. It made me think of my grandmother. There is not any single other entity that ever existed on God's green Earth that I loved more. And I saw her in the lady behind the counter.

"Yeah," I said to her. I put the cash on the counter. She nodded to me, her grin minimized to a subtle smile now, like we were family, which I was grateful for, since it was the only thing I ever really searched for, even though I had already one. Wherever they were.

A YOUNG WOLF

I was waiting in the car outside of work. Windows down. Streetlamp above me. I didn't smoke anymore but sometimes I wished I still did. Off the street somewhere, I could hear music. Hear cars. Hear the city.

Keke came out of the back door in a hustle. He had a big black bag and he lifted the dumpster lid up and swung the bag in. I unlocked the doors and he got in, shotgun.

"My bad," he said, already twirling a dread.

"All good," I replied, putting the car in drive.

"Yo . . . can you take me by Wendy's for that four for four?" he asked me. The way he said it, made it sound like he was just repeating "foe" three times. Thick NOLA accent.

I said, "Aight."

"But listen, can you spot me though?"

I looked over at him, leering. The kid was handsome as hell. Short dreads. He was showing me all his perfect white teeth now. He was slick too.

"I'm giving you a ride home for free *and* I'm paying for your dinner? Fuck you."

"C'mon, man. You see I got my paycheck?" he brandished the slip of paper. "I'll see you at work and get you back."

"Aight," I relented.

There was no line at the Wendy's this late. I leaned back

in my seat when we got up to the glowing menu and let him do the talking. He told the lady over the intercom what he wanted.

"Drink?" she asked him.

"What flavors you got?" he asked back.

"Coke products," she said rather shortly.

"Coke products?" Keke said, laughing. "What that be?"

"Like Dr Pepper and shit," I told him, grinning.

"You want Dr Pepper?" the lady over the intercom asked.

"Nah. Minute Maid."

"Fruit Punch? Lemonade?"

"Fruit Punch."

"Will that be all?"

"Yeah, minus your attitude," Keke said.

"Uh, thank you!" I offered quickly and drove us up to the window. When we got there, a young plump lady was waiting for us. She didn't look too happy.

"Why you giving this lady a hard time?" I whispered to Keke.

"I just got off work. I don't need her blowing her bad vibes my way."

"Well, I can tell you, nobody's working these hours at a fast-food place cause they wanna be here."

"How's that my problem?"

The window opened up and I had my money out for the lady. She handed me the drink first and took the cash. Then she handed me my change, and last, the bag.

"Thank you!" I told her in a voice lighter than my own but the one we all had in our back pocket for such occasions. She closed the window without a word.

As we were driving away, I said to him, "You wanna know the

main reason you don't want to fuck with someone who's serving you food?"

"Man, I just thought about that. You think they fucked with my food?"

I shrugged, grinning again. "I've done it before."

"You've spit in someone's food?" Keke asked me incredulously.

"A time or two, yeah."

"Damn, that's fucked up!"

"It *is* fucked up. You're right. But that's why you don't fuck with people who are serving you food. Because they can get you back like that. And it ain't worth it in the first place. It's not an easy job. You washing dishes. Me making drinks. Kelsey waiting tables. The bosses. Nobody's got it easy. And you never know who's having a hard day outside of work."

He was quiet for a while. I was hoping he was thinking about it.

A little while later, he went, "I'm going on a date Saturday night."

"Oh yeah?" I said.

"We're going to City Park, then going to play laser tag. You think seventy dollars is enough?"

"Yeah, it should be. Not like you're spending money at the park, right?"

"I was going to buy a couple pounds of crawfish."

"OK. And how much is laser tag?"

"I gotta call and ask 'em."

"Make sure you do. Where you meet this girl?"

"She work at the Popeyes around the way."

"Shit. See? How you think she would've liked you talking trash over the intercom like you just did?"

Keke laughed. "Aight. Damn. You got me. Stop bringing it up already."

He had his paycheck out again and was looking at it. "Man, I'm gonna spend this so fast. Cellphone bill. This date on Saturday. Some new jeans. All gone. I gotta make more money. 'Specially if I'm gonna buy a car and move to Texas."

"What you moving to Texas for?"

"I wanna be a truck driver. But I'm only seventeen. You gotta be over twenty-one to drive out of state. So I figure Texas is a big state, a lot bigger than Louisiana. I'll get more work out there."

I got us onto the highway. We passed downtown. The bridge was just up ahead.

"Truck driver huh? Why you wanna be a truck driver?"

"Well, my momma was a school bus driver. At first, I thought about being that. But then I was like, I'll make more money being a truck driver. Drive to all different kinds of places. But also, man, I just wanna get out of New Orleans."

I looked over at him, surprised to hear him say it. "Why's that?"

"New Orleans be toxic, man."

"Toxic how?"

"Just the people. People always fucking with you. More in school. I'm not in school anymore but still. They don't want to see you happy. Sometimes they just testing you, just to see what you'll do, how you'll take it . . . but I ain't with that. I don't gotta prove shit to nobody."

"I hear you. You don't think it'll be like that everywhere?"

"I guess I gotta see, right?" Keke said.

"Yeah . . ."

I pulled off the highway and took the first left. The street curved around, parallel to the highway, and I drove that way a little while before he said, "Take this right."

"How many buses you take to get to work?" I asked him, slowing the car down as we drove down his block.

"Two."

"Damn."

"It ain't so bad. I'm used to it."

I nodded, rubbing my chin with one hand while I steered with the other. Funny, the things we get used to, I thought to myself. "This you, right?"

"Yeah," he said. He had his phone out. "Let me get your number in case I need you."

For some reason that made me smile, but I kept my hand up over my mouth so he couldn't see it. I told him my number.

"What area code that be?" he asked me.

"Virginia."

"You got a nickname?"

That made me smile again. I thought about which one to pick, finally telling him. He just grinned at me, not asking what it was about, just accepting. He had the door open and was standing outside. There was just one streetlamp on the whole block. It didn't seem right. It was very quiet. I couldn't hear anything.

"One more thing I wanna ask you," he said, looking down the empty street, the big dark, no one to see, no one you'd ever want to see, not this time of night.

"What's it feel like, to you, when you the only black mother-fucker at your work place?"

I thought about the question, but not for very long. Maybe at some time that question would have surprised me. And then at another time I might have thought, let me think of something inspiring to say. Something to progress us as black people to the promised land we deserved. That we were owed. That was our destiny.

But what I said was, "You like making money? You better get used to it."

He was grinning again. Baby pearls. He stood there a while, finally nodded, and closed the door. I watched him get to the gate of his apartment complex, get the door open, and then I drove off, back into the heart of the city.

CLOUDS ARE COMING IN

We'd taken this time off cause she wanted to go to the beach. I wasn't really in that stage of my life where a beach was the answer but what I knew was that I wanted to make her happy. It was only a few hours' drive anyway, so why the hell not.

The whole trip there was stressful. The car was buzzing the whole way. Kind of embarrassing at the gas station. I missed the exit by an hour. She'd even called it out to me. I just thought she was being cute. She must not have really believed it either, because an hour later we were crossing into Florida and I'd realized sincerely that I'd missed the exit. I turned the buzzer around and cursed the whole way back. Somehow, miraculously, she managed to remain calm.

When we finally found the place, the tension began to slowly lift. We came up to the counter and there was an overweight redhead with a lot of acne but an honest face. Or maybe she just didn't really have anything to lose, which is certainly a time when a person can be very honest. She told us she could tell we were from way out of town. We didn't live that far away but we were from much much further, so the girl was right about that. We said, It's gotta be nice around here though, right?

She said, "Hell, no. I want to get the hell out of this place."

We got the keys to our room and brought our stuff up and upon entering the room I immediately pulled back the curtains to the window and looked out. There was hardly anyone out on the beach. The sand looked beautiful, completely white. But way off, out over the water, it was very dark.

"The clouds are coming in," I said.

She came over to stand next to me by the window and she put her arms around me.

"The guy at the gas station said it was gonna storm all weekend."

"Fuck," I said.

"It's OK," she said. "This little room can be our get away. This little room is all we really need . . . except . . ."

"Except what, baby?" I said, looking at her. She had these blue eyes. These big blue eyes. I swear to God, you'd be able to see them at the end of a long dream, and they'd be the one true thing you remembered.

"We gotta get some whiskey and soda and some beer and I need some cigarettes," she said.

We did all those things and got back up to the room and it started storming. I was looking out the window again, watching the palm trees bend back. The waves looked relentless. I turned around and looked at my girlfriend on the bed. She was stirring her drink. She was only wearing her panties and a T-shirt with a band that I liked written on it. She caught me looking at her. She smiled. I got into bed.

ACKNOWLEDGMENTS

A number of the stories in this collection originally appeared in the following publications: "Tiger" in *BULL*, "Where Pop Grew Up" in *Coal Hill Review*, "The World" in *Coffin Bell*, "Gattaca" in *Ice Colony*, "Clouds Are Coming In" in *Mind Shave*, "Super Sunday" in *Poydras Review*, "A Cool Cucumber" and "My Friend Ollie" in *Trnsfr*, "No Radio" in *Tusculum Review*.

Thanks to the people who have supported and inspired me along the way, whether our time was brief or built for a lifetime. Thanks to Leena El-Mohandes for your help refining these stories. Thanks to Andrew Blossom for being my river. Thanks to Alban for finding me and giving me this opportunity. Thank you to Lena August for giving me everything. There isn't a way to repay you, but you can add these words to the tab.

Thanks to all the bussers, line cooks, dishwashers, waiters, bartenders, sous chefs, hosts, food runners, and barbacks out there who I hustled along with and continue to. And to the good and fair managers and chefs out there who are too few, salute.

And finally, thank you to Steve Dunn for making a place like Norton Island, for giving the Damned Few and so many others that place and time and those moments. You did good, old boy. Rest in peace.

X.C. ATKINS is an alumnus of Virginia Commonwealth University. This is his second collection of short stories.